I0578887

KENDRAI MEEKS
RELUCTANT
RED CHRONICLES
BOOK 1

ONE

The amber liquid swishing about in Amy's glass tempted both gravity and my nerves. To separate my blonde friend from the bar: a task much easier put to words than action. Side-eying the clock and the bartender's focus on it, I realized last call was nigh. No need trying to liberate Amy's fourth cup of poison from her grasp and shuffle her to our loft to sleep off her drunk. The regulation of liquor sales in the fine city of Chicago would cut her off soon enough. Besides, after the day she'd had, I couldn't blame her for opting for inebriation, even if it did mean I'd likely end up with her slung over my shoulder on the way home.

"Cock-sucking assholes!" Amy's mouth pulled a double shift, vacillating between drinking and spewing profanities that would make the devil blush. "That's what they are, Geri. Every single man is a cock-sucking, fucking shithead. They can't help it, they're *born* like that."

"Not everyone."

I squeezed my eyes shut, refusing to let memory take me. Cody was gone, and there was nothing I could do about it.

"Oh yeah? Name me one – just *one* – who isn't an ass."

Amy didn't know about Cody. *No one* I'd become friends with since moving to Chicago six months ago knew about Cody, or anything much else about my life back in Paradise. The less I talked, the less opportunity for anyone to figure out that the tiny town near the northern tip of Michigan's Upper Peninsula was populated mostly by werewolves and hoods.

Or that I was one of the latter.

"My dad isn't so bad," I offered. "Even if he's willing to give my mom the benefit of the doubt."

Still, I couldn't shield my roomie from everything. She'd overheard enough of the arguments I'd had with my dad on the phone to get the basic gist. Things in the Kline household weren't exactly Brady-like.

Amy blew a raspberry, leaving a mist of her saliva on the counter. "That's only because your parents' relationship is reversed and fucked up as shit. Your mom is the cock-sucking asshole. Trust me, she'd be welcomed at Asshole Camp with the male part of humanity."

Who was I to argue? What little Amy did know of my home life came from me grumbling about my mother's arrogance, or overhearing me argue with my dad in broken Spanish. One day, I thought she'd caught on to my family secret when she'd declared, "I didn't know there were any of your kind that far north."

My kind? What did she mean "my kind?"

"You know, *Hispanics.*" She said the word like some taboo turn of phrase that could launch riots. "Don't worry, I'm cool with it. Besides, I *love* Enrique Iglesias."

I left the comment to air-dry. First, because even though my dad was from Argentina, the rest of my family tree grew from Central and North European roots. Hood society bucked Western tradition by being matriarchal. Brünhild Kline, my mother-and-matron, embraced her Germanic heritage with the ferocity of a bear, and the identity had been passed down to me despite my *papi's* Latino influences. And second, because Amy wasn't rude, she was only socially isolated. Not so different from me. Only, where I'd grown up destined and trained to police werewolves, Amy had grown up on the Upper West Side where labels were openly accepted, if only worn to figure out someone's proper shelf.

As for men, I couldn't really debate Amy there either. I'd only ever had one boyfriend, and that relationship flatlined when I'd walked in on him in the arms of another woman. Come to think of it, Amy might be on to something. The proxy experience, watching a roommate cycle through a catalog of creeps, suggested that at least as far as the localized stock of the student body was concerned, Amy had discovered the only possible explanation.

"Maybe you just suck at picking guys," I suggested, pushing her hair away from where it stuck to her forehead, held in place by a sheen of sweat. "Six months, Amy. We've only lived together six months and this is man number five you've put up as a token sacrifice. You swear you're giving up men for good, and two weeks later, it starts again."

Amy extended a finger. "But this time I mean it. Sick bastard. I gave Carl my heart and my time, and he turns around and starts sleeping with Tiffany Olson!"

"Maybe you should get revenge."

Amy's brow creased. "Great idea. How?"

"By sleeping with Tiffany Olson, of course."

Our eyes met, and a second later, we both convulsed with laughter.

"I should so do that," Amy said when'd she'd gotten her breath back. "Or better yet, pick up the hottest guy here, make the world's longest, dirtiest sex tape, then post it to Carl's Facebook! That'll show him."

Show him everything he and half the men under the age of 30 this side of Lake Michigan have already seen, I thought.

Just as quickly as the idea crossed my mind, I annexed it to that part of my brain I called "Old Geri's Vault." That I'd been raised with out-of-date, uber-conservative values had never eluded me. Even in high school, the human kids—the Hueys, as we called them—had teased the wolves and me about being goody-two-shoes. My clan and their pack had emigrated from the Old Country and set up far from town, in the backwoods. A fabricated ultraconservative church with a Luddite moral code covered for our isolation and odd ways. The fact that we didn't drink, didn't hang out after dark, and never, ever slept around like the other kids didn't make us fit in with popular culture exactly. The truth of it was, sex wasn't the same for us as it was for Hueys. It had consequences. Irrevocable, life-changing consequences.

I threw back the rest of my drink and finished off the tumbler. Four full servings of ginger ale finally resulted in the expected outcome. I slid off the barstool, maneuvered my tiny purse to rest on my right hip, and leaned in towards Amy who stared at her drink like it was some sort of museum display she just couldn't wrap her head around.

"I have to hit the bathroom. You going to be okay here on your own?"

Her reply came in the form of an alcohol-scented belch. Not exactly as concrete an answer as I'd been hoping for, but there was no way we'd cover the six blocks back to our loft if I was hauling this bladder *and* Amy's comatose body.

As for college bar bathrooms at two in the morning, The Old Kettle's held its own. I noted an absence of paper towels and the presence of a chunky, off-white pool on the floor near a wastebasket. The acidic citrus odor of the soap did a good enough job covering up whatever else may be polluting the atmosphere. If I had had a slide or a Petri dish, I'd collect a sample to examine under my microscope out of utter curiosity. Then again, I thought as I counted to thirty while scrubbing down my palms under the hot water, maybe better not to know what hostile chemical concoction I was bleaching my skin with.

I froze the moment I rounded the corner of the hallway and took in the view of the bar, ice coating my spine, my weapon hand twitching. Wearing a saccharine smile and a costume plucked straight out of a copy of *Hipster Goth Quarterly*, the guy at Amy's side pressed up against my inebriated roommate like he was trying to squeeze 'Amy oil.' Apparently, Revenge Plan B had been implemented. Mr. Too Close was probably the hottest-looking thing within ten city blocks, but unlike Amy, I knew he wasn't cruising for a hookup. Not the kind Amy was after, anyways.

The barman and I exchanged a glance. I doubted he was up on the fact that the man creeping my friend was supernatural, but he was clearly picking up on the vibe that he *was* a schmuck trying to take advantage of someone too drunk to break bread with wisdom. I nodded to the barkeep as if to say, *thanks for your concern, and no, there's no way I'm letting him get two steps out of this bar with her.*

"Geri!"

My leggy blonde roomie pulled her hand from the Friday-night Fabio's cheek. Amy waved me over with the enthusiasm of a child seeing a horse at the county fair for the first time. I crossed, shoving my hands in my pockets, and my sarcasm down my throat. When I got close enough, she gave her impromptu suitor a push in my direction, only to pull him back immediately.

"*This* is Donovan, and he's taking me to see some art at his place. He said his car is right outside. He'll drive me home later."

Amy winked, just in case I had suddenly become as stupid as she was acting and didn't pick up on the implication.

"But we came here together," I said, giving Mr. Sexy-Paste-Man the stink eye. I couldn't tell if he was on to me the way I was to him. Vampires were city creatures; my kind stuck to the sticks. "Come on, I don't want to walk home alone. Not at this time of night."

Donovan rubbed a thumb over Amy's inner wrist, the vampire equivalent of swirling a glass of wine before scenting it. "Maybe Geri could join us. With your permission, of course."

His hopes were almost as high as his arching eyebrows.

Amy slapped him playfully on the chest. Dropping all pretense of "seeing art," she said, "Geri in a threesome? *Bwahaha*! Doubtful. Geri doesn't… Well, do anything, ever."

"Ever is a long time. Geri, wouldn't you like to try something, sometime? Perhaps even now? Perhaps, with us?"

Was he honestly suggesting I should lose my virginity in a three-way with my drunken roommate and a Mumford & Sons wannabe? This fangie must be young. Young, and not too bright. In a generous mood, I'd give him the benefit of a doubt RE: his IQ. He might be such a newbie that he'd not yet been oriented towards recognizing a hood when he saw one, or know the danger we held, even if vampire control really wasn't part of our M.O.

I reached into Amy's coat pocket and lifted the little slip of wallet that she kept her ID, student card, and a few dollars in. If somehow the vamp did get her away, I didn't want him to have access to any of her personal things. Despite his earlier suggestion, I knew Donovan didn't have a car. His skinny jeans were so tight I didn't even need him to turn his head and cough to sign off on his physical. There was no way he had space for air let alone a car key in those pockets.

I took a step back toward the bar. "Donovan, was it? You mind if I have just a word with you." With my other hand, I stretched my debit card to the barkeep to cover the tab before jerking my head to the left. The vamp drew Amy's hand to his lips, inhaled deeply, and placed a kiss on her knuckles, coiling her tighter in his thrall.

"This will just take a second. Don't go anywhere."

She nodded, almost frightfully, like she was worried she'd be punished if her butt slid one inch off the barstool. "I won't. I wouldn't." As Donovan turned and followed me, she leaned after him, as if pulled by gravity, almost falling off her barstool in the process.

"Can I help you?" he asked with no amount of hidden annoyance when we gained distance.

I pushed my hair from my eyes. "Yeah, you can, actually. Leave my friend alone. She's already met her asshole quota for the day."

His green eyes shimmered, reflecting the neon lights behind the bar. "I just want to show the young lady a good time, and she seems more than willing. Why don't you do like she asked and take her car home? After that, forget you two went out tonight. You won't notice she's not home until the morning."

I felt fuzz in my brain, an odd mental shake as the vamp tried his best to woo me with his power. It was no more than a brush of a stranger's sleeve against my arm. "Oh, please. You really think your mind control mumbo jumbo will work on me?"

"My…mumbo jumbo?" he repeated, going rigid. "Wait, what?"

"How old are you? A year?" I continued unabated as I browsed his features. "I've always been told your type was into Purple Labels, but you look like you hit up the sales rack at Forever 21. Aren't you Chicago clutches famous for being chic and uppity? A student bar doesn't scream out posh night club or executive lounge to me. Which makes me wonder… Is this your fang mitzvah?"

He winced when I whacked him on the shoulder with the back of my hand.

"It is, isn't it? You really planning on taking my drunk best friend as your first thrall? If she had any idea what you really were, she might be flattered."

Donovan's eyebrow quirked as his cool melted away. "You're not a slayer."

Well, at least he'd finally gotten the clue that I wasn't a Huey. "Of course not. The slayers are all dead. No one's seen one since the Andrew Sisters were hot."

"But, how do you know about fang mitzvahs and clutches?"

Boy, this one's wall of secrets held up like a soggy waffle cone. One or two clandestine facts, and he was fine confirming everything I said. Vamp pickings must be slim in the big city.

"I'm a person who knows these things."

He laced his hands behind his neck, leaned in, and attempted awkwardness. Scratch that, achieved it. "Am I really that obvious? I came on too strong, didn't I? Too much cologne?"

"You could dial back a little, not that she'd be capable of picking up on your scent."

"I just thought, you know, couldn't hurt. Plus, the drugstore was running a really good special on Aqua Velvet."

"It *is* hard to let a deal go by. But if you don't mind, can I tell you something else?"

A hood's training in blade techniques started at age four. I could stab a supernatural before I could write my own name. I threw an arm over Donovan's shoulders while slipping Amy's wallet into a small bag I kept hanging from my left hip, clipped to a belt loop. The vamp didn't know about my weapon until he found my silver blade pressed against the soft flesh between two ribs. His eyes went wide, but luckily, his maker had taught him well enough to avoid making a scene.

"Etiquette would suggest you only drink from a willing partner, and Amy isn't sober enough to agree to a handshake."

"But I'd wipe her memory. She wouldn't…"

"You think that makes it okay? You think fang-rape is okay as long as the victim doesn't remember? Even if that were true, Donny, *I* would know, and I don't forget easily," I said, cutting him off and, well, actually cutting him.

Not that a nick into his flesh would do anything serious. Silver blades wouldn't kill vamps. But a knife was a knife, and making a living kebab of his kidney wouldn't exactly feel like foreplay.

"Take my suggestion and cruise somewhere else tonight. And I better not get word some baby vamp got frisky and left a body. I might not be a slayer, but trust me, my kind is just as much a fan of slicing first and asking questions later."

"And you're not going to tell me what that is, huh? Your kind."

"Human biology major. I also minor in Medieval history, but that's just gravy."

"Geri!" Amy whined when the tab got long and the hours grew short. Not the best timing, when I was trying to be all covert and stuff. "Why are you hogging him? He came on to me, not you."

An atypical Amy argument. Usually, she ranted on incessantly about how I needed a social life that extended beyond our small circle of friends and biweekly telephone calls with my dad that ended in yelling. If she hadn't just broken up with another asshole tonight and she saw me this close with a member of the opposite sex, she'd have high-fived me, shoved a condom in my back pocket, and told me to go ride that buck all the way into town. Hell, at this point, if she saw me making moon eyes at a member of the same sex, she'd probably do a back flip.

Donovan looked back over his shoulder, passing Amy a "just a second, darlin'" smile, but kept his voice directed at me. "I've been casing every bar this side of campus for hours. It's closing time, and if I come back to my maker's place empty-handed, I'm staked for sure. I have to have her. I promise, she won't remember."

"As drunk as she is, I guarantee she wouldn't. Not the point. Get out of here, Donovan. We both know your maker isn't going to stake you over one botched prowl."

"Most makers, no, but my maker ain't most makers."

"Grammar and you don't often break bread, do you?" The blade slid a few millimeters deeper, bringing his eyes and his bile back to me. "You seem to be male, so I assume you have balls. Use them. Tell your maker to get off your back and let you do your first thrall right. Now, I'm going to put my blade away, immediately after which you're going to tell Amy some excuse, then scram. Don't make me filet you; neither one of us needs that kind of attention."

He winced when I withdrew my weapon. I caught sight of a small dark red patch soaked into his shirt as he turned, but the wound would begin to heal in seconds. Donovan crossed to the bar, sending Amy into a flurry of the giddies. She stood up, and just as quickly, fell forward into Donovan's arms. He caught her, proving he might have been a vampire, but he wasn't a complete dick.

Amy's breath carried so much alcohol, even I could smell it ten steps away. She plastered herself to Donovan, playing with what could only be hypothetical chest hairs. "Now, where were we?"

Donovan's nervous smile cracked across his face. He pushed her back onto the barstool. "Sorry, babe. I just remembered I have a big exam tomorrow. I have to study."

"An exam?" Amy asked, wide-eyed. "But tomorrow is Saturday."

"Did I say exam? I mean I have a paper to write," Donovan amended. "Listen, it was great meeting you."

"What? No!" Amy practically broke down crying. She clung to Donovan's shirt, oblivious to the fact that it was ripped and blood-stained on one side. "My worst fears have come true. Geri's frigidness is contagious."

"No, really, I think you're sweet, but… Ow."

This time, my blade pierced his back. Again, only deep enough to be a warning, but he got the point. Literally.

"Maybe I'll see you again sometime."

And finally, Donovan turned to leave, all while shooting me a warning fang from behind a curled lip. Once we were alone, Amy tipped me off that she had reached the angry-drunk stage of the night by poking a finger into my chest and mustering the fury of a methed-up tick mouse. "What in the hell did you say to him? He had the look and everything!"

My eyebrow quirked, amused that my sweet, free-love, upbeat roomie thought she could sustain bitterness for more than a blink. "The look?"

"Of course, you don't know the look. No one ever gives you the look. You don't let them get so far as a smile," she prattled as I signed the slip the barman pushed across the counter and stowed my card. "You know, the *look*. The one that says a guy wants nothing more than to take you to the nearest bed, strip off all your clothes, and spend the rest of the night making you scream."

Maneuvering my arm around Amy's back, I spun her toward the door. Even though she was three inches taller than me, I bore her weight without any difficulty. Hoods were stronger than humans. Even without having gone through my formal rites that would awaken all my strengths and abilities, my innate gifts still made hauling a society girl's drunk ass out of a bar after last call a breeze.

"Take away the bed and the stripping all the clothes off part, and I think you've just described the effect I have on every man lately."

"I know, and it's so Sandra Dee. My god, have you ever even kissed a boy?"

I blushed, pushing back bittersweet memories. "Yeah, a few."

She blew a raspberry, covering the side of my face in 40-proof spittle. "I mean like, a full on, I-want-you-right-here-and-right-now type of kiss. Not a peck on the cheek in the church basement." Amy was convinced every person who'd grown up in what she called the "in between places," i.e. not the East Coast and not the West Coast, spent their weekends in Bible school or shooting grizzly bears.

She continued without waiting for an answer. "Don't you ever get tired of studying all the time when you're not in class or working out? Of only ever having a social life when I force you to? Why are you always such a good girl?"

"Sex has consequences, Amy. Especially where I come from."

I felt a hitch in my breath in the shade of the memory. *No,* I lectured myself, moving Amy along faster. *You will not go there. It was doomed from the start, and you knew it. You knew it could never work.* "I'm really not that pristine; we just have different definitions of what bad behavior entails."

"Maybe, but my way is the best way." Amy fell against me as we left the back alley of the bar. The front would be safer, but after last call, it would also be lousy with police looking to make the city a quick buck, fishing out of a barrel as the bars emptied. We got six steps from the door when the world changed its spin.

I looked like a mime trying to rationalize the sudden appearance of a box around me, grabbing at empty air. Amy was gone. Just gone.

TWO

Instinct took over. There was a hunt afoot. Only this time, my prey wasn't a two-hundred-pound werewolf. It was a hipster wannabe who, maybe, soaking wet could make one-twenty. Donovan may have been a baby vamp, but I'd never taken on one of his kind. Would my skills for hunting wolves transfer to hunting a vampirical barfly?

The perpetrator must have been waiting in the shadows; under street lamps I'd pick him out in a blink. The alley, bathed in stripes of fluorescent and gray, took on definition as I honed my vision. The nearby garbage bins provided the assailant with a robust olfactory cover of stale alcohol, cooking oil, and filth. Mixed in the miasma of stench and rot, however, was a very distinct, fresh overlay of cheap cologne and disappointment.

My ears would hear the scratching of mouse feet in the ceiling if there were no other background noises, but this environment wasn't like my family's compound back in Michigan. A few hundred meters away, plastered frat boys and let-it-loose coeds tramped down the street, cackling and wailing. If Amy had been struggling or resisting Donovan's assault, I might stand a chance, but there was nothing. Either she'd blacked out from alcohol, or she'd blacked out from a vampire's knock on her noggin. Either way, I was operating blind, which would make rushing in with fists flailing stupid.

My mother had tried to get me to train for the possibility of facing a vampire someday. I drew the line at knowing ten ways to kill a werewolf. If I ever told her my best friend had died because she'd been right and I'd been wrong, I'd never hear the end of it.

Plus, you know, Amy would be dead. Despite her many, quirky flaws, I really liked my roomie.

Luckily, I had read a little bit about vamps and their abilities. There was a wide river between things a vampire really could do, and what the movies showed. Fly? Not really, but even a baby vamp could set Olympic records in the high jump. Turn into bats? No. The really old and powerful ones could become a cloud of smoke to get out of tight pinches and traffic tickets. One skill they had which Hollywood never picked up on was a form of vocal stealth. Hiding in the shadows wasn't much of a defense against hoods, let alone slayers when they were still around, since our better-than-nifty hearing could effectively echolocate. Either by some magical power grab or evolutionary dumb luck, they had developed the ability to throw their voices, making it impossible to pin down their location just from the sound.

"Come on, Donovan. You know how this ends, right? Hint: it rhymes with 'shmule be read.'"

He refused the bait.

"Amy?" I called into the void, hoping if she was still conscious she'd at least moan. Even with her offline, the sound bounced off nearby objects and filled in some of my blind spots. To the left of me was something large – maybe a dumpster. My eyes adjusted to the dimness, letting me in on a little more. Black bags and boxes that had been piled up until they made a barricade of grease-drenched cardboard lay on my right. "Come on, Amy. It's late and you're drunk. Let's get you home."

Donovan's voice, somewhat mottled by what I was willing to bet was an emergence of fangs since last we spoke, sent a shiver up my spine. His comical and desperate display in the bar made me forget the truth: even a baby vamp could kill.

"Just leave, witch. Your little 'leave my friend be' speech and knife was real admirable, but do you know how much they're going to bust my balls if I show up without a thrall for my own initiation ceremony for the third night in a row? I'm not going to kill her. I just need her to be my first feed."

"One, I'm not a witch. There's no such thing as witches."

At least, as far as I knew.

"And two, you don't have to kill her to screw her up. Or didn't you know thralls can leave residual headaches, nausea, night sweats, and delusional obsessions for up to two months? Amy already gets all that from watching reruns of *Full House*."

"What, you think you're Web MD or something?"

"I'm thinking of applying to medical school."

Donovan croaked a laugh. "Yeah, you obviously got that bedside manner thing down."

Keep him talking, Gerwalta. As long as his mouth was busy spitting back retorts, he wasn't sinking his teeth into Amy. True, he'd want to wait for his ceremony, but if what he said was true and it had been three days since his maker cut him off from secondary feedings of his own thralls, he could be getting bloodlusty and stupid.

Time was running out. I needed to draw him out, kick his ass, find Amy in the shadows, and get her home. Problem was, *he* didn't need to engage *me*. One well-timed leap, and even dragging an unconscious or struggling body, he could outmaneuver me and escape. The only advantage I had was banking on a weakness of many a baby vamp, or hell, most college-aged men: a male ego.

"Take off, bitch. You know you can't take me, and you know enough about us to know we don't kill anymore."

"You're asking to abduct my friend and feed from her on the honor system? Fine, take Amy. Let's see how much they bust your balls when they find out you had to force her to go home with you. All your vampy charm and Jedi mind tricks, and you can't even pick up someone on a college campus infamous for loose women."

That did it. One moment I was alone, and the next, Donovan was a foot from me, huffing in my face. Only, no Amy. No best friend. She couldn't be too far away, but I was still going to have to chase him off or leave him a whimpering pile of vamp goo to search for her.

My training had drilled into me that I should never, not even for a millisecond, look away from a supernatural opponent. A vampire or wolf within striking distance was a creature within killing distance. Then again, I had been pretty avidly ignoring my upbringing and training since I'd run away from home, and apparently, my mind saw no use in kicking in now.

One quick glance over his shoulder in hopes of seeing Amy in the shadows was all it took to find myself a foot off the ground, Donovan's hands around my neck, and me, choking.

The pubescent vamp sneered, his dark intentions bubbling at the corner of his mouth. "My maker said I couldn't kill humans, but that don't save you, does it? Lucky for you, I'm curious. Tell me what you are, tramp, and maybe I'll make your death quick."

My mother's voice screamed inside my head. *Willful, wistful, foolish child! In the heat of battle, the enemy does not care about your bloodline or your wish for diplomacy. The only thing that will save you and anyone you're trying to defend is your ability in combat and your training!*

I wished I was stronger. I wished I'd listened to my mother more and trained harder, instead of going through my "trying to be a normal person" phase. I wished I hadn't run away that night six months ago, when my mother had commanded me to finally take my rites and my rightful place in the clan. Couldn't I have just stuck around one more day, threw myself into the ceremonial fires to burn away my human coil, and gained all my powers? A vamp whose fangs hadn't fallen yet was outdoing me; I couldn't get my fingers winched under his grip on my throat. Was this how I was going to die? With Amy suffering and, even worse, my mother thinking she'd been right about how wrong my actions were?

No, I had to prove her wrong, save Amy, and, most importantly, save myself.

Remember your training. Look for his weaknesses.

Donovan's weaknesses? His ignorance about what I was, and the fact that he could apparently be prodded in the ego with such ease.

I gasped enough air to get out a few words. "Maybe I'm a wolf."

He pulled me right up to his face, and inhaled. "Don't smell like wolf to me."

How would he know? Given the fact that clutches pretty much stayed in the cities and packs in the countryside, I didn't see how.

"So unless you're prepared to tell me what you really are," Donovan continued, "and why I should let you go…"

He never got the words out.

Donovan whipped around, trying to figure out where the empty beer bottle that had smashed into the back of his head came from. It sent a spray of glass shards everywhere, and if he hadn't effectively become an inhuman shield, my face would have been cut to shreds. The glass couldn't penetrate a vampire's skin, of course, but the tall, lumbering idiot at the far end of the alley probably didn't know that.

"Hey, arsehole!" the man called, his voice sounding like an extra from some dry British comedy. "Didn't your mother teach you not to choke women in an alley in the middle of the night?"

Backed by the glow of the street lamps, our interloper looked like a life-sized cutout of a WWE wrestler. The stranger was on the taller side, and either was wearing a full set of protective football gear or had been endowed with the muscles of a Greek god. Broad shoulders pared down to a surprisingly slender waist. A body Amy would have called "a swimmer who'd I like to see up close doing a breast stroke."

But as the wind shifted, carrying his scent on the breeze, I knew that this triangular muscle mass over sturdy long legs also described another type of male. A bristle of recognition went down my back and I squeezed my eyes shut. Why didn't I sense him a long time ago? Or had I? Suddenly, the lurch in my stomach when I'd come out of the bathroom made more sense. I was a hood; the nearness of a vamp shouldn't have any physical effect on me.

The nearness of a werewolf, however…

"Take a walk in the other direction, dude," Donovan said without turning, his clenched jaw and fangs roughening the edges of his words. If he knew how easily the werewolf could snap him like a twig if he wanted, he'd be running. "This doesn't concern you."

What the hell was he doing here, and why was he by himself? Lone wolves were rare, mostly because of how imbalanced they became the longer they stayed away from their pack. Was he one of my mother's informants? He wasn't a member of the Paradise pack; I knew each one of those wolves by sight and smell in either of their forms. I supposed he could just be in town on vacation; most wolves didn't like to travel too far from home but it wasn't entirely unheard of. Would he walk away and leave me to the vamp, once he figured out what I was? The wolves where I came from were respectable members of the community, but this *wasn't* where I came from.

"Actually, I have two rather compelling reasons to be involved," the wolf said, taking a few steps forward. In a dictionary-inspired rendering of the term 'cliché,' he held up both hands and made fists. "I call them Pain and Abel."

Without a second of difficulty in keeping me pinned, Donovan pivoted toward our guest. "Seriously, get along, little doggie."

Great, so the vamp did know. Well, that just made this already complex situation even more so. Looking over Donovan's shoulders, I opened my eyes and tried to pin the wolf with a glare.

"Go," I begged.

The Brit took two more steps, but the interplay of shadow and light still cloaked his identity. "Look, hood, I'm not all keen on helping one of your kind, but an honorable man does what he can. It's not your call."

"A hood?" Donovan appraised me with fresh eyes. Despite that, his expression curdled. "But they're all out in the boondocks."

Exactly one of the reasons I chose this school over all the others. Still, since my cat was out of the bag (side note: what kind of sick bastard kept cats in bags?), I might as well use it to my advantage. Able to find focus and, you know, breathe, I sucked in oxygen, directed all my energy to my legs, and called on my innate abilities for all they were worth. With one triumphant *harumph*, my right foot connected with his balls.

I fell to my feet as Donovan doubled-over.

"*Biiiitch*," he hissed out, looking up at me from his wounded-manhood stance. "Now I'm going to – *ooooouuuucchh* – kill you!"

With another maneuver that I'd mastered at the age of eight, my knee slammed into his stomach. Donovan hit the ground, and I hit the darkened regions of the alley, looking for Amy.

The wolf drew near, but I didn't think he was stupid enough to get too close to me when I'd just flat-floored a vamp in two moves.

"What are you waiting for? Run."

"That vamp took my friend into the shadows. She's probably passed out. I got to get her out of here before she wakes up and sees a man with fangs."

He pointed absently at Donovan. "Toast him, then, and get the hell out of here."

"Glean the context clues, O Ye of the Moonies. I'm trying to stay under the radar. Toasting a baby vamp on the evening of his fang mitzvah doesn't exactly aid in my incognito-ness."

"Why are hoods all so self-centered?"

My back went rigid. I paused long enough to fix balled fists on my hips and give him my full attention. Mistake. The moment my eyes met his, my knees decided to become conscientious objectors. Such fire, such heat. So much like Cody had been when fired up about something. Still, I managed to pull off a good impression of a righteous bitch.

"Our job is to police wolves. Vamps don't fall under our jurisdiction."

The wolf took two more steps in my direction. Instinctively, my hand went for my weapon, and to the pouch on my belt loop that contained it, only to find it had fallen off in the melee. I knew I should have woven the blade into my hair like usual.

"How can you say that, after what he just did to you? Your kind should be doing something about it. *You* should be doing something about it."

"That kind of decision lays with a matron," I spat back. "In case you haven't noticed, I'm still a nascent."

His brown eyes narrowed on me, rimmed by a glow of green. A vein on his temple pulsed. My mouth went dry. Was he going to wolf out right here? I got lucky that Donovan was a baby vamp; my training – and, fine, the wolf's intervention – was enough to take him down, but I couldn't take on a fully-grown wolf if he wanted to attack. Especially without my silver blade.

He must have picked up on the itch of fear tingling under my skin. A smug half-smile pulled up his lip. "Frightened that I'll eat you, little red?"

My eyes went wide. *Little red.* Was it a coincidence, or did he really know about me? Resolving to reacquaint myself with my spine, I turned back to the task at hand: picking up dripping bags of filth and throwing them behind me. "I don't have time for this. I have to find my friend."

The next pile of garbage I budged moaned. I dived in, finding Amy, conscious but confused, under what looked like an old smoking jacket.

She put her hand to her head as I pulled her to her feet. "What the hell happened?"

It was that moment I was faced with the dilemma: make my already depressed roomie feel even more depressed by telling her she'd been attacked? That the "making her scream" Donovan promised involved forcibly sucking her blood, or…

"You passed out."

…lie to her face.

"I did?" Amy surveyed the nearby shuttering stack of clothing and regret that was Donovan. He keened in his pain, trying to force himself to stand erect.

After how hard I'd kicked him, any kind of erection on his part was going to be hard to come by.

Amy pointed vaguely in his direction. "Is that the guy that was trying to pick me up?"

"Yeap. He tried to bully you to go with him when we came out. You kicked him in the junk so hard it made you pass out."

Amy sobered in 3.2 seconds as she turned toward the street. "And who's the hunk?"

Hunk? I turned, thinking that she might be confusing brawn for beauty, and found myself struck dumb. Now that I had a second to consider the wolf at leisure, I saw what had Amy's radar beeping.

One thing that Hollywood got wrong, was supposing that every supernatural creature was also a supernatural sex bomb. While some were cute, it wasn't inherent to the status. Some were, frankly, ugly as sin. When I looked at this wolf, sin would definitely be part of the description, but more along the "inspiring carnal thoughts" variety.

Standing about six-two, he was just the right combination of muscle and lean sinew. His skin tone and skeletal structure suggested his pack was likely, like my mother's bloodline, descended of the Northern or Eastern European stock. It fit the accent. Like many wolves, his deep brown eyes bordered on black, hiding under bushy eyebrows that, despite the field day they'd present for any beautician, somehow complemented what was probably a persistent five o'clock shadow. In a pair of fitted jeans, a worn denim jacket, and an old pair of work boots, he had country boy charm down to a tee. If not for the fact we were creatures separated by tradition and sanctions, I'd be howling at the moon myself.

As if sensing the question in my eyes, *how do you want to play this, wolf?,* he took the initiative to cover our tracks.

"Passing by and heard a ruckus," he said.

Amy stepped right back into I'm-willing-and-available mode. She was a sucker for accents. And anything cute with a penis.

He continued, "Wanted to be certain you were okay. Plenty of bad blokes in this part of the city. Never know who or *what...*" He winked at me. *"...*you may come across."

Amy examined him with drunken eyes and sweetheart dreams. "I'd say. Hey, do you want to…"

With a jerk, I pulled Amy along, rushing her past the still seething Donovan. "Thanks for your help," I said, not even turning to the wolf as we hurried by. "Got to get her home. Like you said, all kind of *bad blokes,* and unfortunately, that's her favorite kind."

Present company, not excluded.

"Thanks for the help. Next time drinks on me, okay?"

"Jello shots off his stomach!"

"Amy!"

THREE

The hungover Huey's bedroom door didn't even crack open until almost 2:30 in the afternoon, though at least she had managed to shower before reintroducing herself to the world of the living. Clutching fistfuls of wet hair, she leaned against the frame of her door and stared at the ground.

"I think I was doing shots of Mack truck last night."

"With Sherman tank chasers," I confirmed.

I'd gone over the usual vamp strike zones the second we were secure in our loft the night before. No puncture wounds. Nothing but a few light scratches. Donovan hadn't in fact penetrated her during those few moments in the shadows. I wasn't really sure what I'd do if Amy had been bitten, but I'd need a better story than 'you passed out' to explain the damage.

Sitting at the kitchen island on a highboy stool, I offered her the cup of coffee I had been refreshing for the last three hours, anticipating her need. "Now that you're sober – well, *soberer* – want to talk about the breakup without the assistance of alcohol?"

She shuffled with the grace of a Teletubby. "I think all I'm capable of at this point is moans. Thanks for the joe."

Amy called coffee joe. I had a feeling it was an East Coast thing, but I couldn't be sure. I'd never been to the East Coast. Outside of a few trips to the Black Forest and occasional ride-alongs with my mother into Southern Ontario or Minnesota, I'd never been anywhere. Even the trips to Germany weren't exactly illuminating. All kids born to the House of Red went straight from the airport to the ancient hunting lodge that served as the ancestral home of our line. A month annually, starting at age seven and until such time as your bloodline matron determined you were ready to receive your rites.

When I'd first met Amy, she was as exotic to me as if she'd been from Brazil or New Zealand. The native New Yorker probably thought I was just as weird. Me, unassuming Gerwalta Kline, a junior transfer bio major from a tiny little drive-thru town with a population of less than 500. Never mind the fact that of that number, about a quarter were Yooper Werewolves and a few hoods in charge of policing them and the other dozen packs of their kind spread around the region.

Plus, there was the fact that I'd achieved the age of twenty-one and had never slept with a man, which in Amy's world, put me in ranks with Bolivian knife-throwing clowns for rarity.

She assumed the stool next to me and reached across for the package of bagels and the tub of Nutella I'd left out. "The breakfast of champions, hey?"

"Depends, champion what?" I sipped my own coffee, long since cold but what the hell did I care. "You don't want to talk about it? Fine, but I will. How many times are you going to go through this cycle? No man is worth that kind of self-abuse."

"Said like a true virgin," she teased. "There are some men who take a lot more than a drunk night to get over. But don't worry, Geri. This pounding headache and I have learned our lesson. No more dating losers for a while."

I tapped her on the shoulder as I rose to take my empty mug to the sink. "Good to hear you're not giving it up completely."

"Why would I, when the world is rife with mistakes I could still make? Speaking of which…" Amy leaned over the island, grinning. "Did you get his number?"

"Whose number?"

"You know. Tall, dark, and happened-to-be-passing-by last night."

I picked up my plate and pivoted for the sink. "No offense, but I don't think dives-into-an-alley-at-closing-time guy is a romantic prospect."

"Who said anything about romance? Come on, Geri, you can't tell me that even you didn't notice how hot he was. And the way he was looking at you? It was like he wanted to gobble you up."

Gobble me up? It had been a lifetime since a wolf had actually attacked and eaten a hood, but it didn't make the possibility any less real. But that wasn't what shocked me. Truth was, I was dumbfounded by Amy's selective memory. How could she recall such detail about one glare, but when it came to remembering being swooped away by a vampire and thrown in a pile of garbage? No, on that she drew a blank.

"No, I didn't get his number."

The anticipation that had been bubbling in Amy's expression went flat. "His name?"

"Not that either."

She ruminated a moment before shrugging. "Doesn't matter. A man doesn't look at a woman that way unless he's planning on sleeping with her or killing her. You two had a moment. I bet you it's not the last one. Do you really not want a boyfriend, or have you somehow convinced yourself that you're not worthy of one?"

A chill went down my back when I remembered the wolf's intensity. Between sleeping with me or killing me, I had a definite fix on which was more likely. Besides, I'd already dated one wolf, and I'd learned the hard way why that was such a bad idea. Even though I'd been named after the infamous Little Red Riding Hood, didn't mean I'd make her same mistakes.

My nose wrinkled. The snide little reference the wolf made the night before still irked me. Did he really know I was of the House of Red, or had it been complete chance? Did he know that my mother, in a willful attempt to rewrite history, branded me *Die Verräterin*'s namesake?

Amy's quizzical expression reminded me that she was still expecting an answer. No, I did not think the wolf had been tasty, but I did think he signaled trouble.

"What can I say? I'm sexy. I know I am. It doesn't mean I'm going to hop every bus that comes along, just because I think it might be fun to go downtown someday."

"I swear, you're going to force me to hire a himbo just to get you laid."

My eyebrow raised. "A *himbo?*"

"Yeah, you know. A male bimbo? Not her, but a *him.* A *himbo.*"

She stated this all like it was obvious and common. What did I know, it might have been. I hadn't exactly been raised in anything approaching Huey-world culture. Even the humans in Paradise weren't exactly on the forefront of fashion and culture.

"Sorry, but we don't have many *himbos* back in Paradise."

Amy huffed. "I swear, you come from one of the most inappropriately named towns ever." She ticked off its shortcomings, all learned through me of course, on her fingers. "No shopping, no spas, no coffee shops, no life!"

"There's always life, Amy. It has many variations."

"Spoken like a biology major," she deadpanned. "Look, I'm ordering you, if you see Hunky McHunk-Hunk again, bare minimum you are to get his name, his phone number, and his eye, okay?"

"Not okay. Trust me, he's not my type."

My roomie planted two balled fists on her hips and a grimace on her face. "I swear the sacred pinky swear of roommates that I am going to see you actually using that body of yours for something other than gym abuse and as a book-transportation implement before we graduate." Then realizing what she'd just said, her rigidness faded. "Not, like, personally of course. I mean, I'm not actually going to watch you do it. Seriously, though: name, number. You think the universe just throws a man like that into your path at random?"

No, I didn't, and that's what scared me. In general, wolves were rural folk. Part of the reason I had wanted to come to school in the big city was the fact that the nearest pack was seventy miles to the northeast, in a forested region along the Illinois-Wisconsin border. No wolves meant there was also no hood commune nearby. The last thing I wanted to do was have a regional oberst, who no doubt would report straight to my mother, think I was now in her territory and therefore, at her disposal.

Which resurfaced the question: what was a British wolf doing in Chicago anyway, and was he really alone, or did he have a pack nearby?

I didn't know which possibility frightened me more.

I decided I'd been on the pointy end of Amy's knife long enough, and turned the conversation back to her. "You still planning on going to the library, or can you not yet walk straight?"

"Why wouldn't I be able to walk straight? The only guy I spent any time with last night was Jack Daniels."

"You got in a few words with Johnny Walker too."

A sizzling sound permeated the air as Amy sucked in breath through clenched teeth. "Yeah, Johnny… He does things to a girl, you know. Problem is, she usually doesn't remember it afterward." She scooted off the barstool and grabbed an apple from a bowl on the counter. "Library. Supposed to meet my study group at five-thirty. It will be getting dark then. Damn it, I hate walking across campus after dark on the weekends. I always feel like I'm being followed."

FOUR

Amy had been gone for all of ten minutes when I felt it.

Deep in my gut, the curl of recognition. My arms broke out in gooseflesh. Hoods had a certain innate ability to detect when a wolf came near, especially in isolation. Last night I'd probably felt it, but I'd been distracted by the vamp. Now, in my own apartment and preoccupied with nothing more than a blog post on nitrates, I couldn't help but notice when my insides twisted.

Even though the modern, scientific brain didn't want to believe it, there was something mystic in the universe. I'd seen it time and time again. Hell, my family was living proof. After going through the ritual that we called the Gate of Fire, a fully initiated hood had powers that lay beyond the borders of rational reason. Even a nascent, like me, could hold her own if she played her cards right.

Amy had entertained me when I began putting little silver objects around the flat. A city girl not familiar with the occult, she swallowed the "these are the trinkets of my people" excuse. She accepted it as Bible truth, not even asking which people. The fact that my lineage was from Germany and Argentina suggested I probably wasn't dancing around wigwams as a child. One of the first lessons my mother had taught me was that anything could be a weapon, if you threw it hard enough and had good aim. Even a tea tray, and in particular, a silver one.

It had to be him. There weren't enough wolves in Chicago, especially in my area, for it to be coincidence.

I put my ear to the door. A slow, measured inhale, exhale, inhale, exhale. My grip on the tea tray handle tightened as I mentally charted the consequences of my options. Should I open the door and immediately whack him across the head, or rip off the handle and try to shove it into his chest? Silver always hurt a wolf when they came into contact with it, but the only way for it to be lethal was if it touched the heart or brain. As a nascent, my only hope of coming out of an attack unscathed was to be on the offensive.

Strike last, die first, as my mother would say.

"You know that I know you're on the other side of the door, right?"

As stupid as I felt, I actually shuddered when his baritone brogue erupted. "How?"

"Because I'm a wolf, and you're a hood, and that's how it works." I could practically hear the smirk in his smug voice. "I know you're a nascent, but are you completely ignorant? Or are the wolves where you come from as incompetent as you?"

"Of course not!" Then, realizing how I'd just been cornered into demeaning myself, I guffawed. "I mean… You know what I mean! Were you tracking me last night? Did you send the vamp after my friend to flush me out? Trying to make me scared so I'd go running home?"

"I literally have no idea what you're talking about." Through the peephole, he embodied the art of disinterest. "Believe me, I'm about as happy at our running into each other as you seem to be. Why I didn't just walk away still niggles at my brain. One less hood in the world sounds perfectly good to me."

Jesus Christ, what was his deal? Traditionally, hoods and wolves weren't best buds, but we usually maintained a healthy amount of respect where the other was concerned. At least, where I came from we did. And, if you took "respect" to mean, "We hoods will leave you be as long as you act nice, but step one claw out of place and we will silver your ass."

"Why bother then?"

"Did you want to be murdered by a vamp, or are you just into kinky stuff?" He laughed wryly, running a hand through a head of hair distorted by the peephole to look conical. "I didn't come up the alley to save you. I was worried about the Huey. But while we're on the subject, can I just mention that, usually when a man saves a woman's life, she's grateful? She might even say thank you."

"You're not just a man, and I'm not just a woman. Now tell me why you're here."

"Are you looking through your peephole?"

I pulled back, feeling like a kid caught with her hand in the cookie jar. "No."

"Oh my God, hood. You have to be the most annoying type of your kind. Look, I don't know why you're in the city, and I don't know why you're living with Salty Two-

Tits as a roomie. I get the feeling she's not exactly aware that she's living with a wolf-slayer or that she almost got sucked on by a parasite last night. I'm just trying to do the right thing." I heard the rustle of cloth and a shifting of his body from left to right. "Look through the peephole. I mean, again."

A small, rectangular piece of plastic with STATE OF NEW YORK printed at the top replaced his head in my line of vision. Amy's ID stared back at me.

"Both you and your friend dropped your bags in the alley. I figured you wouldn't want the vamp to know where you live."

My mind raced for other explanations. "How do I know you haven't attacked her as she walked up the street just now, and that her ID is all you have?"

"So your theory is I somehow magically knew what building you guys lived in, and was just waiting for the rise of night to empower me, so I could get her ID and find out the exact unit, because *that* level of detail proved too much for me?"

Sarcasm was a tongue in which he was obviously well versed. Still, I didn't believe him. Amy had gone to the library to meet her study group. Without a student ID, she'd be unable to get in.

Just at that moment, I felt my cell phone buzz in my back pocket. Taking it out, I read the message from Amy on the screen.

Got all the way to the library and realized my wallet isn't in my bag. Do you know where I left it last night when we got home?

Such timing was the work of a cruel and bitter god.

"Let me guess, that was her asking if you knew where it was. Am I right?"

"No need to be smug." As I spoke, I sent Amy a message, telling her she'd left it on the kitchen counter. Best not to let her know the truth. She'd be convinced the guy on the other side of the door had tracked me down because he was desperately in love with me after just one glance and that I should take him to bed posthaste. "Leave it outside the door. I'll take it when you're gone."

"Tobias."

Maybe my hearing was failing me. "What?"

"My name is Tobias."

"I don't do quid pro quo with strange werewolves. I'm not telling you my name, and I'm not opening the door while you're here, so just go already."

"You want me to huff and puff, then? Isn't that how this goes?"

"That's the Three Little Pigs, not Red Riding Hood."

"Right. I get the two confused, seeing as they both just show wolves to be evil, when it's really the hoods who are to blame for most of our problems."

Loyalty to my lineage, drilled into me over a lifetime of training, upbringing, and genetics, battled with good judgment. *He's just trying to get you emotional so you'll open the door to confront him without thinking. Then he can attack.*

"No comment on that?" he asked, amusement coloring his words. "Illuminate me, then. What is a nascent hood doing here, all on your lonesome, in an area without wolves? Something tells me this is that famous American teenage rebellion I've heard about. Giving your matron a little scare before you fall into line and become part of the system? Fine, then. Then I'd guess that you're not skirting about Chicago on any sort of official business. In which case, what cause would I have to hunt you down?"

"Yet, here you are," I answered. "And I could ask you the same thing. What's a wolf doing in Chicago, and a British wolf at that? Wolves hate cities."

Rather than answer, Tobias changed the subject. "You got something silver ready to bludgeon me with?"

"Of course I do. I'm not stupid."

"Big words for a girl who, just last night, was nearly strangled in a back alley by a vampire," he said. "I have questions, questions you may be able to answer. I'd prefer to be face to face to ask them. If you're lying to me, I'll see it in your expression. If it takes you silvering me for that to happen, so be it."

My eyebrows rose. "You're volunteering for me to cause you pain? Who's into kinky stuff now?"

"It will heal in a few hours if I don't hold it too long. If it gets me answers, it's a small price to pay."

I had questions too, ones only Tobias could answer. Temptation to take him up on his offer made a nerve in my temple twitch.

"I don't have silver thread. I mean, I do in my bedroom, but…"

"And we're back to the kinky stuff. Okay, as you're not about to wander away from the door for fear of me busting in and chasing you on the way to your chambers, that won't do, will it? What are you holding then?"

I looked with shame and self-ridicule down at my hands. "A tea tray."

He swallowed a laugh. "Because I'm English? Trafficking in stereotypes, I see. Fine, open the door, and we'll trade. I'll give you the two bags, and you hand me the tea tray. It should drain enough of my energy that I won't be at my full strength. You could kick my butt with a feather."

"My fist would do."

"Holding silver, I believe that may just be true."

I closed my eyes, inhaled deeply while calling on my innate abilities, put my hand on the door and…

Under the humming light of my building's hallway, I could see he was definitely the kind of wolf that could devour an unwary hood. Taken individually, his facial features seemed harsh. A strong chin, slightly ridged brow, glass-cutting cheek bones… But when taken as a matched set, they did him well. If one of the Hemsworth Brothers and Gaston from *Beauty and the Beast* had been able to procreate, Tobias could have been their miracle offspring. He stood taller than me, like most mature male wolves, so that he found himself looking down on me. In a literal way, that was. But given the way he was glaring at me, Amy's purse and my tiny bag outstretched at arm's length, the metaphor didn't fall far behind.

I lifted the tea tray in kind. Each of us mirrored the other when our free hands reached for what the other offered. The moment I had the bags in hand, I let go of my silver. Tobias hissed as his fingers closed around the tray's handle, and the burn began to take hold.

I backed back into my loft and reached for a nearby display of collectible spoons on the wall. The silver didn't have to be large or weaponized to be dangerous. Sometimes, a momentary distraction was enough to outsmart a wolf.

Tobias followed me in, looking at me with twinkling eyes. "Is all your silver in the form of kitchen implements? First the tiny little paring knife in your bag, and now this?"

Even though I doubted anyone living in my building would care, I closed the door as he entered. "It's a dagger, not a knife. And FYI, it was forged by my great, great grandmother."

"And so tiny that, in essence, it's just a fancy knife. Nevertheless, I have no interest in attacking you, or making any use of your tea tray, mini spoons, or – I'm guessing the next thing will be candlesticks?"

"This is my house, so I get the first question." Amy's purse and my bag went flying as I tossed them on the floor. "Did you tell anyone about me after last night?"

"Um, no. Did you tell anyone about me?"

"Who would I tell?"

His sarcastic, dry laugh curled my stomach. "You'd report me to the closest matron."

"I don't give a flying pheromone what Chicago's *orbest* knows." His mild rebuke reminded me of my years of training. Years that now seemed wasted, as I had no intention of ever carrying on my family's legacy. "Just curiously, though, does she know you're here?"

"As if you didn't check one of your big brother databases. The people who really need to know I'm here do, so don't worry your pretty little head over it."

I narrowed my gaze on him. "If you're passing through, that wouldn't have been in the records when I last looked. But *why* you're passing through – that's a different question. So tell me, how is it you strolled by last night when I just happened to be nearly attacked by a vamp?"

"One," he enumerated his retort on the fingers of his free hand. His other hand kept a grip on the tea tray. "He didn't nearly *attack* you; he nearly *killed* you. Something, incidentally, you still haven't thanked me for preventing. And two, I believe it's my turn to ask a question. Had you ever seen that vamp before?"

"Not unless you count inside the bar about ten minutes before, when he tried to pick up my friend."

"Right, your friend, Amy. Isn't it weird that I know your friend's name and not yours? If you're going to silver a pup, the least you can do is throw him your moniker. At least then he knows whose name to include in the profanity-laced curses when he's tending to his blisters later."

"Fine. My name is Geri."

He quirked an eyebrow. "Your mother a fan of Mick Jagger's exes?"

"Doubtful." If he wanted a name, I'd give him the name. "It's short for Gerwalta. But *everyone* calls me Geri."

"Your mother doesn't."

I almost sent the spoon flying right into his temple. Had it been my dagger, and had not Amy been due to arrive any moment to get her purse, and that she'd likely notice a mortally injured hulk of a man bleeding profusely on our living room floor, I would have.

Instead, I did the next best thing. I glared. "How do you know that?"

"A hood names her daughter after *Die Verräterin* herself, I'd wager she's got a lot of rep and expectation vested in that name from the get-go." He tilted his head to the side, taking on a canine-like manner. "I hit the nail on the head when I called you Little Red, didn't I? But I thought Chicago was under the control of a House of Yellow."

"The Matron of this region is of the House of Yellow, and not exactly Red's biggest fan. She's - none of your business." Let him take a swig from his coffee pot on that one. "You swear to me you just happened to be passing by? Nobody sent you?"

"You swear you're just here, doing the college thing, and nothing else? You haven't been sent here to chase down leads?" he countered.

"I also take a pottery class on Saturdays, if you must know." This time, it was my turn to be confused. "Wait, leads? There are no reports of supernatural problems in the city since Al Capone's days. And while we're on the subject, how did you know I was a college student?"

"Because I'm not a Luddite." When I just returned a dead stare at him, he rolled his eyes and continued. "Amy talks about you on her Facebook page. I wanted to know if she was hiding something I should be aware of, being that she fraternizes with hoods."

I crossed my arms. "And?"

"And I don't think Amy hides anything. Ever. Just FYI: if you're trying to stay on the down low, you might want to ask her to stop trying to hook you up. What's with that, anyway? Can't you handle your own love life without outsourcing to Manhattan Barbie?"

I made a mental note to talk with my roommate again about my *media mentions* request. Of course, Amy being Amy, she attributed part of my single status to the fact that I wasn't "swimming where the sharks feed." She had no idea the type of sharks I was trying to avoid. The daughter of Brünhild Kline, the Matron of the House of Red, would be a pearl in some dick's collection.

In my silence, Tobias continued. "Three pieces of advice, little red. First, splurge for quality."

Tobias put the tray down on a nearby coffee table. When he pulled away his hand, I noticed only the slightest tinges of red on his inner palm. Holding on to a silver object for so long should have at least given him second-degree burns.

"There's not enough actual silver in this thing to give me watery eyes, let alone neutralize any of my strength. Two, given who your roomie was trying to go home with last night, I wouldn't exactly trust in her judgment when it comes to men. And three, you should know there are vamps in this area, even at your school. Be careful. I'm not saying they're necessarily all bad, but if you're going to be in the practice of performing S&M with them in dark alleyways, I'd at least carry some gold around."

"Gold?" I asked.

"Yes, gold," Tobias repeated, putting extra emphasis on the hardness of the g. "Or don't you know that it has the same effect on them that silver does on us? Bonus advice: get actual gold. Pyrite will leave you feeling slightly foolish."

"Haha, because it's fool's gold. Are all British wolves so funny, or are you a special case?" I deadpanned.

One jab in just the right spot in his ego was all it took. In a moment, we went from standing several feet from each other, to breathing each other's breath. The air whooshed from my lungs as Tobias's hard body pressed against mine. His canines had grown long in the space of a blink, and were mere inches from my nose. His eyes shone like golden orbs, like the eyes of the dog he was when he connected with his animal nature. When he spoke, the sound was distorted, the human words struggling to be formed by a lupine mouth.

"There's very little about this that's funny, hood. Understand? If you get in my way, I will end you."

Adrenaline pushed my pulse into marathon speeds. I struggled to bring the silver spoon still in my grasp up to touch his flesh, but Tobias dominated my every inclination. I couldn't move. My state must have triggered his instinct, and he leaned in, running his tongue over the pulsing jugular on the side of my neck.

Click.

We both turned moments before the door opened. Amy bounced in, as if she had found total sobriety and a Red Bull sometime in the last twenty minutes.

"Hey, Geri, I…. Oh!"

There were unspoken subplots and devious insurgent conclusions in that grin. I knew what it looked like: me with my back to the wall, Tobias's body covering mine, his mouth hovering at my throat. To Amy, this was a finally-making-out-with-a-guy session. To me, it was a barely-getting-away-with-my-windpipe-intact session.

She lingered at the door, beaming at me with the pride of a deviant mother seeing her daughter don a miniskirt for the first time. "Well, well. Lookie here. Hello, stranger. Even through my drunk, I knew you had a thing for Geri. I hope, Geri, you got his name, like we discussed."

Without giving Tobias a chance to speak, and cutting off any prepubescent schemes born of one Amy Popowitz, I pushed the wolf away from me and toward the door. He was too busy pulling back the effects of his partial wolf-out to raise a hint of protest. Also, my spoon might have been pressed into the sensitive skin over his wrist as I forced him by the hand through the room.

"It's Tobias, he was just leaving, and he's never coming here again. He does, and I'll call the cops."

As I shoved him past Amy and out the door, I added, "And you know exactly the type of cops I mean."

FIVE

"Has he called?"

"Being that I didn't give him my phone number, he might find that difficult."

"YOU DIDN'T GIVE HIM YOUR PHONE NUMBER?! Are you *insane?*"

"Not enough to give my phone number to some random guy who first, is hanging out in dark alleys in the middle of the night, and second, is all creepy-stalkery and randomly turns up at my apartment the next day."

"You realize, allowing for slight variation in the details, that you just described about half of the romantic comedies from the 1990s, right?"

I turned on Amy, expecting to see her grinning at her joke. Instead, what I got was a hybrid expression that melded genuine concern with the pity one reserves for idiots.

"You also realize," I said, "allowing for a slight variation in the details, that also describes about half of all unsolved murders in, like, every decade, in the history of the world, ever, right?"

My roomie was not pleased. She shook her head and clicked her tongue like a seventh-grade teacher who'd just caught one of her star students spraying graffiti all over the lockers. For some reason, Amy had decided that I was to be her acolyte, even though I'd told her – though honestly, I didn't give a damn – that I didn't want to complicate my life with guys. Besides, what would happen if I did meet a guy I liked? One of my kind's edicts had been dutifully drilled into me since grade school by my mother. "In our blood is our survival. Outside our blood is our death." Then, as an afterthought, she'd add, "Don't forget what happened to the slayers."

Of course, *that* was impossible. I couldn't not forget what happened to the slayers, because I didn't know what happened to the slayers. No one did, not really. Oh, sure, there were theories on why they'd disappeared. The leading one, the one to which my own mother subscribed, was that their elders had allowed too much marrying and coupling with humans. That was, that slayers bred themselves out of any meaningful existence, producing children whose innate talents weakened with each succeeding generation. At some point, their offspring wouldn't have been strong enough to take rites and become initiates in their community. "City folk," she added with a huff. Too much opportunity for the heart's distraction. Hoods, in her opinion, did well by keeping themselves in communes, limiting involvement with Hueys.

That implied that slayers —and for that matter, hoods —weren't human. Collectively, supernaturals had decided at the advent of genetic testing that such concrete evidence of our existence would be bad. Because of that, I had no proof that we all were, as I suspected, some type of Huey. Then again, if *Die Verräterin* had managed to bear a wolf a child, hoods and weres had to be at least related closely enough for it to be possible.

"This conversation is done."

Gathering my books from the counter, I slipped them all into the backpack along with my keys, wallet, and cell phone. I ducked into the bathroom long enough to slip my dagger, its blade only two inches and its hilt appearing to be no more than a fancy hair clip, into the black braid that roped half way down my back. After what happened in the alley, and after having nearly lost it when I dropped my bag, I wasn't going to be without it for quite a while.

"If you see Tobias, you are to give him your phone number! You hear me, Gerwalta Kline? I have a feeling about this one!" Amy called as I made for the door. "You could see it in his eyes when you pushed him out. That man is on a mission, and you are his objective."

Chicago's weather seemed like a practical joke concocted by a bitter god. I'd expected rain, cold, snow, sleet, sun, and its infamous winds at intervals. After six months, I was still getting used to experiencing all of them during the twenty-minute walk from the loft I shared with Amy to the biology building on the WCU campus. Our saying in Michigan was, Don't like the weather? Wait five minutes and it will change. Chicago weather catered to a clientele that thought that was just too long to wait.

WCU, of course, varied from its infamous and more prestigious city-serving cousins. It wasn't the University of Chicago, and it most certainly wasn't DePaul or Loyola. Most importantly to me, however, it wasn't the dinky community college a half-hour drive from my family's compound, and therefore wasn't a den of mother's spies, who'd report back on any "mischief" I got up to unfitting of the next great hood in her illustrious bloodline.

That I was here still seemed a miracle. My mother had not held back her cackling one iota when, after graduating high school two years before, I'd said I wanted to go away to school. There were no degrees in Hood Studies, and no university in the world offered a course on Lycanthrope Diplomacy and Treaty Negotiations. It was only my father's intervention that allowed me to enroll at community. When it'd come time to transfer or finish my associates, I embraced the old saying, better to ask forgiveness than permission.

The Matron of the House of Red would never have given her permission, and as yet, she sure as hell hadn't mustered up the ability to forgive. At one point, I thought she might never speak to me again. Then I realized I'd never actually be that lucky.

I'd submitted the WCU application in secret and managed to use a small inheritance from my grandmother and savings from a part-time job to cover the first year of tuition and living expenses. Transferring as a junior had plusses and minuses. Plus: I didn't go through all my freshman foul-ups in front of the very same professors who were now mentoring me. Minus: everyone else in the program was already established with a lab partner they'd been with for two years, meaning in an odd-numbered class, I worked on my own without any help.

I double-checked the procedures for the exercise of the day and measured my chemicals with military precision. Wouldn't my mother be proud I'd found some activity that benefitted from the high standard she'd held me to as a child? After twenty minutes or so, I was scribbling notes in my lab book when I felt the presence of someone behind me.

"Casper must really be helping you out today."

I turned and stared at the sweet, aged face of Prof. Hikimoto.

"Sir?"

He took a seat next to me and pointed at my experiment. "You've gotten to step twelve when most of the class is still lingering on step seven. It's hard to believe you've done this on your own. I was thinking, maybe there's a ghost working with you."

"Ghosts can't interact with physical objects. One wouldn't be much help to me."

His face blanked. Finally, he decided I must be joking, smiled politely, and continued. "Your labs are executed with precision and thrift, your test scores are at the top of the class, you have an amazing sense of maturity and self-reliance… Tell me, Miss Kline, you wouldn't be looking for a job, would you? One you might continue on with full-time over the summer?"

I scarcely kept myself from hissing. I may have pulled off my dramatic escape late last fall to sneak off to school, but I hadn't yet considered where that left me when classes got out. I supposed I'd still have my room in Amy's loft; the sublease I'd signed had been for twelve months. But was I going to just hang around Chicago and bide my time? It wasn't like I could go home again.

I shrugged. "Haven't thought about it much. Why?"

Prof. Hikimoto pushed his glasses up his nose and blinked three times rapidly. "A colleague is seeking a few student candidates for a project. It starts as part-time for the rest of this semester and turns into full-time come summer."

"An internship? Like a job? Would I get paid?"

He sheepishly smiled. "You wouldn't be making a lot by any means. But if you were open to doing something that would gain you some industry experience, get you something you can put on your resumé to impress any future employer, I think it would be a great experience."

Future employer? Résumé? It suddenly occurred to me that my glorious rebellion against my mother and the seemingly born-to eventuality of becoming a sanctified hood didn't have to be some sort of late developmental temporary state. I could actually run with this and build a life for myself. I could get a job. An actual job, with a supervisor, paid vacation, dental insurance, sensitivity workshop trainings… and no werewolves.

The inheritance I'd gotten from my grandma and my savings wouldn't last forever, after all. Eventually, I'd either need to retreat home with my tail between my legs, or make my own way in the world. Given the choice, I'd go with the latter.

"I might be interested."

"Oh, wonderful!" Prof. Hikimoto clapped his dry hands. "I'll let Prof. Karmarov know. He's already working with one graduate student on the project, and wanted another. I told him he'd be a fool not to consider you though. He'll get in touch with you about the details. Keep up the good work, Miss Kline. I see good things in your future."

My future? I'd heard the phrase since I was knee-high to a scratching post, but always in my mother's rumbling and demonstrative prognostications. She'd more than expected greatness from me for my own benefit; she demanded it for her own. For our family's. For our *legacy* and *legitimacy*. We were the House of Red, the most prominent hood bloodline in the world, with the most ancient roots, and the one to whom other hoods deferred.

We were also the ones with the biggest humiliation to live down.

"A mother hood names her daughter after Die Verräterin herself, I'd wager she's got a lot of rep and expectation vested in that name from the get-go."

The memory of Tobias's instigation played at the back of my thoughts. Most particularly how he'd chosen to use the word "vested." My mother wanted all the bloodlines to know that she was not only the Matron of the Red Hoods, but that she could rewrite the legacy of our biggest shame by branding a name that had become a curse on her only child.

But I'd turned my back on my mother's attempts to rub clean the cloth of our history, and engrave one of her own using me as the pen. I renounced my birthright, and with that, I'd unmoored myself from the harbor of my destiny. It had all happened so suddenly, I'd never stopped to pause and consider all the opportunities now open to me. An internship at a real company, working for real people, making real money (okay, a small stipend), for real work? It sounded too good to be true.

I walked home on cloud nine, grinning ear to ear and absorbed by the tunes filling my earbuds. Butterflies did a cha-cha in my stomach, anticipation over all the things that could come of this mounting sense of self – a self that wasn't defined and confined by some mystical birthright. Maybe that's why I didn't recognize that in that cloud of butterflies, there were also wasps buzzing. As I dashed across a shortcut back alley on the way between the campus and the apartment I shared with Amy, my pursuer took advantage of my distraction and isolation.

One moment I was shaking my butt to the upbeat song beating in my ears, wrapping a scarf around my neck.

And the next moment, I was kissing my ass goodbye.

SIX

A bitter, familiar taste nipped my tongue. Blood. *My* blood – hot, sticky, and free flowing in a rivulet down my face and across my lips.

Had I bitten off my tongue when I'd been jumped from behind and my body, flattened against the urine-washed blacktop? Taking account of my senses, calling on my innate powers to aid in my awareness, I realized the truth was almost as bad. Crude, long fingers threaded my hair, forcing my right cheek to the ground but giving me a view of my assailant's own head next to mine. A sharp pierce of pain just behind my left ear pulsed, and what blood released at the point of a fang that didn't get immediately sucked up by the vampire flowed down into my own mouth.

"Get off of me, asshole."

My futile demand fell silent over the detritus around us. I recognized him, of course. Donovan, the vamp from the bar. He'd probably been following me since that night, just waiting for a chance at payback. And here I was, a pretty little package of distractedness. How could I be so freaking stupid?

Another deep pull of my blood into his mouth, and I felt the first flirtations with dizziness and pain hit. He was draining me like he couldn't finish the deed fast enough. That's when it hit me. He wasn't just trying to fang-rape me. Donovan was out to kill.

I struggled again, trying to free myself. "I'm warning you, last chance."

His lips, pursed around the wound his teeth had bolted into my neck, curled into a smile I could feel, but he still didn't release the hold.

As I called on all my strength, readying myself to buck him off of me, hoping he didn't take a bite-sized chunk out of my neck when I did so, a rumble permeated the air. Like a sheet of ice, it covered both me and the vamp, and we both went dead stiff.

Looked like someone was about to cut in on my and Donovan's dance again.

The vampire's jaw slacked moments before an arc of fur and teeth knocked him off of me. I scrambled to my feet to find the vamp, who moments before had been grinding my face into asphalt, in much the same position. Only instead of a humanlike creature with its devilish hand forcing his head down, it was the maw of a huge red and black wolf, its teeth on his throat and its massive front paws on his shoulders, pinning him to the asphalt.

I pressed the raw flesh behind my ear and pulled back to find a trickle of blood. The moment the wolf took out my adversary, my body had redirected all my innate strength to healing itself, as if by instinct. I still didn't understand why hoods were gifted in this way. Beyond wielding silver and the few of us that could fly, we didn't have what many Hueys would refer to as "super powers." What we had were human abilities, amplified. Like the Six Million Dollar Man, I was stronger, faster, better than human. Only, as a hood who hadn't completed her initiation rites, I could only be superhuman in a very subpar way.

"How now brown cow? Or should I say, red wolf?"

The wolf didn't loosen his hold of Donovan in the slightest. Instead, the muscles over his eyes shifted, the lycanthrope equivalent of raising an eyebrow.

"You're not going to kill him, Tobias. If you had wanted to do that, he'd be dead."

"Get your damn dog off of me!" Donovan attempted to squirm, but he had about as much luck with that as an elephant squeezing into a tube top.

"*My* dog?" Approaching my would-be murderer, I shifted my weight and sent my foot flying, catching him in the s, sending a sickening, bone-crushing crack echoing off the alley walls. "One, he's not mine. And two, are you really that ignorant that you don't know a werewolf when he's trying to subdue you?"

"Of course I know he's a werewolf!" Donovan bit back. "And I don't care what you are. As soon as this mutt gets off of me, you're dead. Do you know what I got for coming home without prey on the night of my rise? Sixteen effing minutes of sunlight!"

"Sixteen, huh?" I asked, mocking him with fake awe. "Well, that is a very particular number. You must have been very crispy when you went back inside. But judging by your supple, baby-smooth skin, I'm guessing you got your fangs on someone since then. So my question is, did you kill them?"

His tongue peeked out of his mouth, smearing across his bottom lip until a fang stopped its path. "Not yet, but you'll be dead soon enough."

A punch of incredulity hit me in the gut. Even the wolf swayed a little in that.

"My blood?" I said. "My blood healed you that quickly?"

"Who knew?" Donovan asked. "My maker says hood blood is better than Neosporin for us. Told me not to come home until I had drained you dry."

Immediately I knew what I had to do. And I hated it. Hated it with a capital HA.

Pushing up my sleeves, I called on my gifts to embolden my strength, even though the effort halted the healing that had already reduced the pulsing and gushing behind my ear to a dull trickle.

"Let him go, Tobias."

The wolf removed his maw but kept his body planted atop the vamp. His head cocked to the side in a way that almost made me forget he was a wolf. He looked like an adorable puppy hearing a high-pitched noise.

"I'm ready." I nodded, reinforcing my statement. "Let him up on the count of three, okay? One, two, three…"

Several things happened all at once. The wolf leapt, landing soundlessly four feet away – far enough away to give me a window but close enough to spring back into action if I needed him. At the same time, Donovan shot to his feet like a spring daisy. He pivoted with a speed my brain could barely follow, and barreled right toward me.

And then there was the third thing that happened. Me, angling my body and shifting right in time to jump up on Donovan's shoulders, thread my fingers through his hair, and twist.

Body and head flew in opposite directions, each landing with a thud a few feet away. I, however, came down in a perfect crouch, one hand before me to steady myself on the pavement.

Tobias shifted back to his human form, showing me respect by not assuming his nudity would be in any way bizarre. I'd been witness to the naked human forms of wolves of every size, shape, and color since I could remember. There was nothing seeing this one's perfect male form was going to do to me.

Well, at least not with him six inches from me and his finger driving into my collarbone.

"What the hell, hood? You killed him?"

Confusion deformed my expression. "Um, yeah. Wasn't that the plan?"

Tobias's jaw worked. "Did it ever occur to you to rough him up for information first? Maybe query *why* a vamp saw a nascent hood as such a threat? Or, bloody hell, even ask who his maker is, in case he sends another of his mosquitoes after you?"

Now that he mentioned it, it was a little odd. And if I was a fair person, I'd admit that to Tobias. As it turned out, in that respect, I was my mother's child after all.

"One of the primary guidelines I've been taught since I was a child: deal with an immediate threat before worrying about the greater implications."

"So shoot first and ask questions later. Yeah, you're *definitely* a Red."

"What exactly do you think he might have said? Come on, Tobias, it's obvious. He failed his initiation rites. He didn't get a thrall home for his ceremonial induction. His master commanded him to come after me because he wanted him to die, but didn't want to do it himself. I've read stories about vampire justice. You wouldn't believe the consequences."

"I'm guessing the fact that *you* killed him doesn't make those consequences magically go away, does it?"

A lump in my throat threatened to cut off my ability to breathe. Holy shit, no it wouldn't. There were procedures for this kind of thing, protocols. Ones I wasn't familiar with, but that my Matron would be. What I did know was that any maker worth his salt would be seeking recompense for the loss of their child.

Which meant, in a very short span of time, my mother would know I'd slain a vampire. Even if they didn't know I was the Red Matron's daughter, and even if they didn't know my name, word of such things spread through the community like disease. As far as I knew, I was still the only hood in Chicago. That left little room for scapegoating.

My nerves made me go on the defensive. "I was justified. He pledged to kill me. You heard it! If I get called out for this, you *will* witness for me."

"I don't think the testimony of a lone wolf will count for much, do you?"

"You're in Chicago alone?" Were his words ever going to stop punching me in the gut? "How long have you been away from the others?" I held my breath, waiting for his answer.

"Only two weeks."

The rush of air from my lungs carried away some of my anxiety. A lone wolf, without a pack, would eventually go insane. He'd kill without hesitation. My father, a hood of the House of Yellow, had told me tales that still turned my stomach, of tracking lone wolves gone over the edge across the Pampas, and destroying them.

"You've got a few months then. But why is a lone… No, you know what, none of my business. I don't want to be involved."

"Neither do I, and yet, here I am again," Tobias said, running a hand through his hair.

"Speaking of which, how did you end up here this time? You really going to tell me that you just happened to be walking by again?"

"Of course not. I've been tracking his scent since that night outside the pub. He's been following you for two nights, just waiting for when you'd be stupid enough to walk down a dark alley. You know, Gerwalta, I've saved you twice now, when really, letting that vamp toast you would have worked out better for me by a long run."

"Well, then, if you ever chance upon me being attacked by a vampire again, please, don't hesitate to go fuck yourself."

His hands tightened into fists, and for a moment, I thought he was going to hit me. Instead, they just shook at his sides.

"Ungrateful, entitled bitch."

He turned on his heel, lashing his fists into the empty air. When he turned back, I saw the wolf flash in his eyes. Maybe he'd been out on his own longer than he'd claimed. He was already displaying irrational behavior.

"If anyone does come asking you about what went on tonight, you mention one tiny little thing about me, and I will track you down to finish what the vamp started. No one except you knows I'm here. I'd like to keep it that way."

"I'm not exactly going to be shooting off fireworks to let everyone know I nearly got my ass kicked. If you're fine with me taking all the credit, works for me."

"Go ahead. I don't need my ego stroked. And, just so we're clear, this is the last time I'm helping you," he ground out. "So, please, for fuck's sake, don't be an idiot. Lighted roads, no more back alleys. I told you, there's something going on around here with the vamps. They might not fret over hoods in general, but now that one of their babies kissed pavement while out on assignment to tick you off, you'll be on their radar. If they're anything like the vamps where I come from, they're really into that vendetta thing."

Lacing my arms over my chest, I shifted my weight from one side to the other. "Don't suppose you're going to tell me just where that is, will you?"

He answered with a finger pointed In my direction. "I mean it, Gerwalta. Next time, you're on your own."

"Fine by me!"

I barely got the words out before a ripple of fur shot down his chest and over the pulse points around his body. Wolf-Tobias gave me a flash of his sharp canines, the werewolf equivalent of passing me the middle finger, before turning and exiting the way he'd come.

Leaving me alone in a dark alley, with a decapitated vampire corpse.

SEVEN

As a hood, my primary area of study and training had been on how to work with – and when necessary, against – werewolves. That was our purpose. My *abuela*, who lived with us briefly before her death, told me that God had to balance the world when he created supes, all to protect his ultimate creation: man. Wolves ruled the wilds and vamps held dominion in towns and villages. He created hoods and slayers as the buffer between them both, and between the Hueys with whom they shared territory. Slayers were to vamps as we were to lycanthropes: an intermediary between them and civilization and when necessary, if one ever got out of line, a bringer of punishment.

Hoods weren't meant to balance vamps. As I looked down at Donovan's headless torso and torsoless head, I knew why. My stomach threatened to vie for an Olympic gold medal, it was turning so many flips. How could there be so much blood in something that wasn't technically alive?

I looked at my phone. 1 AM. The sun wouldn't be up for hours. Would I have to wait till then for the body to dissolve? Would it dissolve? Or did it explode? I suddenly realized that you could drive a semi truck between the margins of what I knew and what I thought I knew. There were no vamps in the Upper Peninsula. I'd have to go clear to Detroit or over to Green Bay to meet one if I ever got the notion. Realizing I needed advice from someone I could trust, I plopped down, took out my cell, and sent a message to my cousin.

You don't know anything about vampire corpses, do you?

Markus took a painfully long time to answer. *I think I saw them open up for Metal Trap once. They really rock.*

Not a band. Actual dead undead.

Academic interest or practical application? :/

Chest heavy, I sighed and keyed in my answer. *The latter.*

A nanosecond later, my cell rang. In the silence of the alley, the soft trill became Gabriel's horn. Hermes would drip with envy over the speed of my answering.

In my mind's eye, I saw my cousin's herculean frame overtaken by his friend-of-Dorothy mannerisms. "One, where the hell are you? And two, why?"

"Why what?"

"Don't get smart with me, little red." Markus clicked his tongue. "You know perfectly well why."

"I'm in Chicago. I'm going to school here." A fact my mother and father knew, but probably hadn't shared with the family due to shame. "The vamp was trying to kill me, so I sort of just, you know, killed him first."

"*You* killed a vamp?"

I didn't know if I should be proud or offended at the surprise in his voice. "I had a little bit of help."

"But there are no other hoods in Chicago. At least, there's not supposed to be."

"It wasn't a hood that helped me." My voice and my courage shrank. "It was a wolf."

"There aren't any of those either!"

My hand slapped over the receiver, hoping to cover up Markus's shouting. A moment later, I did my best to explain.

"There's at least one. Markus, you can't tell my mom, okay? You can't tell anyone. He's saved me twice, and I really don't want to pay him back by getting word to the *oberst* that he's around. I'm keeping an eye on him. If he gets out of hand, I'll let someone know."

"Are you seeing him? Are you *sleeping* with him?"

"No, and on that note, you should really meet my roommate. You both seem to be overly concerned with my love life. Can we focus on the problem I'm currently having? I need to know about vampire corpses. I know you had some kind of weird obsession with the vampires once. Tell me what you know."

My cheery cousin turned adamant professional. "Method of death?"

"Decapitation."

"Current location?"

I side-eyed the body. "About three feet from me. We're in an alley. I thought they just sort of fizzled when they died. Or melted, or something."

"They're vampires, Geri. Not the Wicked Witch of the West. Are you somewhere that the sun is going to hit when it comes up?"

The alley ran parallel to a street I knew from staring at maps ran east to west. "If there's sun. It's supposed to rain tomorrow morning."

"Doesn't matter," Markus said. "Even if the sunlight is diffused, the body will still turn to ash. It will just take a little longer. Rain would be good, in fact. It's going to wash away all the dust. Of course, you're probably going to want to take all his clothes off."

"WHAT?"

This time, it was my voice that threatened to give me away.

"Think about it, little red. Even without a body, if someone comes upon a set of clothes and shoes laid out like someone deflated inside them, it might draw attention. Make sure to get rid of any identification he had on him too. Now, go on. Strippy, strippy. I'll wait."

"Don't dare ask me to send you a picture of this."

"I'm gay, Geri. Not a necrophile."

Resting the phone on a nearby box, I got to my feet and did as my cousin advised. While true that naked werewolves didn't make me blink twice, something about defrocking a near stranger made me curl my lip in disgust. The smell didn't make the process any more tolerable. Every item removed perfumed the air with Eau d'Vamp, a sickly sweet smell, like tar-covered caramel. When Donovan's body was nude, I picked the phone back up.

"Okay, I did that. Now what?"

"Now, you wait for sunrise. Your fingerprints are all over his stuff. Anyone comes up to him before dawn and calls the cops, you're screwed."

"So you actually just made this harder for me. Thanks, Markus. That's great. Jesus Christ, how did the slayers deal with this crap? Vampires live in cities. They couldn't have just been babysitting undead corpses until sunrise all the time. Someone would have caught them."

"The slayers didn't have to wait," Markus said. "They could conjure sunlight. All they had to do when they killed a vamp was throw a solar flare at it."

"Great for them."

I felt my hackles rise when a noise at the far end of the alley caught my attention. Looking up to where moonlight hit shadows, I caught sight of a slowly trudging silhouette. The way the body shuffled with small steps and rigidity told me it was neither a vamp nor a werewolf. The labored slide-step-slide could mean it was a zombie, even though I was pretty sure those didn't exist.

"Shit, I have to go. Thanks, Markus. I owe you one."

"You mean you owe me one more."

With a click, he was gone.

Donovan's bewildered eyes and mouth, stuck in a last rattling of his favorite cuss word, sat flash frozen in his bulbous head across the way. The person at the far end of the alley stopped, leaned over a trash bin, examined a couple of random objects, then moved on to the next.

I could run for it, but like Markus pointed out – slash that, *ensured* my prints were all over the scene. Nope, I had to stay here and see this through, even if it meant improvising.

When Amy had extolled the joy of giving head, she probably hadn't pictured it quite in this way. I pulled off my loosened, blood-soaked scarf and pawed for Donovan's head. It didn't exactly want to stay in its original position, i.e, at the end of his neck, continually rolling like some partially deflated basketball. Finally, using my scarf, it kept its position, the fabric covering the gap between his *cabeza* and his lower faculties. Taking a breath and ignoring the vomit trying to crawl its way up my throat, I threw a leg over his bare hips and settled myself over his midsection.

As the homeless guy made his way up the alley, nothing more likely to get him to turn and run occurred to me than if he caught us "in the act." Only, after a moment of my theatric gyrations and faux moaning, I realized instead of running away to avoid the gooey awkward of apparently finding two people mid-coitus, he kept his eyes fixed on us.

I froze.

"Don't stop." He shuffled his hands, as if telling me to run with something. "I ain't gonna intrude, just want to watch."

I huffed. "It isn't a public show."

The gruff, grimy man waved a hand through the air. "Not with all your clothes on, it ain't. And your guy doesn't seem to be helping much. Isn't he stiff or something?"

I perused the corpse beneath me. "Oh, he's stiff. And of course, I have my clothes on! It's only forty degrees out here!"

"If you were doing it right, you wouldn't care." Then, turning to Donovan's head, he said, "Never learned to please a woman, have you son?"

And it was at that precise moment that the vampire's noggin rolled out of the scarf.

I moved before realizing I'd made the choice. I was on my feet and had a fist into the man's temple before he had time to do more than raise a hand and bring the question to his lips. If I needed more reasons why I was going to Hell when I died – starting with breaking that whole commandment about honoring thy mother – rendering an innocent albeit voyeuristic homeless guy unconscious was adding to my ledger.

Screw due diligence. I grabbed my things and turned tail for home.

EIGHT

Amy refused to believe that I hadn't actually gone out and "got my v-chip revoked" when I hadn't come home until two in the morning. The night we sat and watched a movie with a no-holds-barred love scene, however, finally changed her mind.

My face morphed into a mask of disgust as the camera zoomed in on the ridiculous facial glitches of the couple as they went into rapid bunny mode. "Is that actually what it sounds like? I don't think I'm going to be able to keep a straight face when the time comes."

"If you come, you won't." She giggled, making a pretzel of my words. "You weren't lying, were you?"

"I generally don't. I *avoid* the truth on occasion."

"Fine, you didn't track down Mr. Hot and seduce him. But if you weren't, you know, with someone, what were you doing?"

I'd regurgitated my rehearsed excuse. "I told you, I got sleepy working late in the lab, put my head down to rest a few minutes, and woke up six hours later."

Technicality number one: I had gotten sleepy in the lab. I just didn't fall asleep there.

"Right, you fell asleep in the lab. Oh, Geri, did I tell you what I got in the mail today?"

I paused in my attempts to down another handful of popcorn.

"My birth certificate!" Amy squealed. "Which is awesome, because I thought it'd take two days at least, you know, given that I was just born yesterday."

"Ha ha."

She rose, taking the bowl of popcorn with her. "Fine, maybe you just were dry humping or fish facing. Or maybe you went all *Breaking Bad* and spent the night cooking up meth in the chem lab."

"We don't do that kind of stuff in organic chem, Amy. It's more like plant cells and stuff. A little genetics, if we get really crazy."

"At this rate, you're going to be a virgin until you're sixty."

I batted my eyes. "Don't you mean, sixty-nine?"

A beige throw pillow became a beige *thrown* pillow as Amy chucked it my direction.

"You're hopeless, Geri. Hopeless!"

We'd only gotten to the awkward morning-after scene in the movie when there was a knock at the door. My hand when to the hilt of my dagger in my hair, even though I didn't sense any wolf nearby. Being attacked by a vamp raised my vigilance. Amy was already to the door, however, her hand on the handle.

"We live in a big, bad, dangerous city, Amy. At least look through the peephole!"

Amy rolled her eyes at me, but still did as asked anyways. "Good call, Geri. Thank god I didn't open my door before making sure it's only a delivery guy."

In the hall stood a nondescript man wearing dark clothes and holding a clipboard.

"I'm looking for *Garwalter,* um, *Girvalter…* Kline, a Mister Kline?"

Amy reached out her hand expectantly. "Gerwalta, and that's her," she said, jerking her head to the side to indicate me on the couch behind her. "You need a signature or anything?"

"Oh, I'm…Sorry, *Miss* Kline. I've never heard that name before. It's very…"

"German." I completed his sentence for him, getting up to take the pen and clipboard. "It's an old family name. Is this it? You just need my signature?"

He nodded, holding out a standard-sized envelope. "Actually, no, I need an answer too."

I looked at the envelope as though I expected it to explain. "An answer to what?"

The delivery guy shrugged. "Not sure. I don't ask the questions, I just follow the orders. I can wait out here. You can close the door if you want. I won't go anywhere."

My mind raced with possibilities. Was my mother trying to get to me through an intermediary since I'd refused to answer her calls? Was Markus following up on my predicament, and doing it in an unusual way to throw off any suspicions of his own mother? Had I won the lottery?

But the last thing I expect was what I actually found. A letter penned elegantly on fine ivory linen paper.

Miss Kline,

I received your information from Prof. Hikimoto, who recommended you as a candidate for the special research project I'll be running this summer, which also includes preliminary lab research this semester. Yamato-san's rave review of your tenacity, intelligence, and performance in his class is encouraging, but it has been my experience that it is always wise to meet and discuss these things in person, in order to review the expectations we both may hold, as well as to discuss compensation. Would you be able to visit me at my office, Browning 359, this Wednesday evening at 8:30 PM? I do apologize for the late hour, but this project is being conducted in what I understand most people refer to as "free time," and our current hours generally run roughly 8 PM to 11:30 PM, twice weekly. (Another consideration before accepting the position.)

Please respond with haste, ,
Prof. Igor Karmarov

Amy, reading over my shoulder, wrinkled her nose like she'd smelt something foul. "Sounds weird, Ger. What kind of professor asks to meet you at his office at eight-thirty at night, and expects you to work until almost midnight?"

What kind of professor, indeed? My stomach developed a lupine-shaped lump.

"Plus, come on… Igor? Seriously, his name is Igor?" Amy said when I hadn't responded to her original comment. "Does he have a hunchback too?"

"Igor is actually a very common name in certain parts of Eastern Europe." *Like the parts with the biggest of the Old World packs.* "Just because we associate that name with creepy literary characters doesn't mean they do. I heard the name Adolf is even making a comeback."

"It shouldn't. And moms shouldn't name their boys Igor. That's just cruel. Why not Sven? Isn't that Eastern European?" Amy's fingertip drew a line over her lower lip. "Mmmm, Sven."

"That's Scandinavian. But, having grown up with the name Gerwalta, I kinda get what you're saying. It's always sad when people chalk up too much to a name."

I fetched one of my lab notebooks from the kitchen table where I'd been studying earlier and scribbled a reply, before ripping out the sheet and folding it in half.

"Here." I stuck out the sheet to the courier. "Thank you for coming out this late. I really appreciate it."

The courier tipped his head. "Seems to be the only time of day Prof. Karmarov asks us to do anything, ma'am. It was no problem."

NINE

Browning Hall had been built at a time when Gothic architecture was the everything-old-again-is-new-again thing. I felt like I was walking into a military academy, entering under its hatched brick towers and angular windows. A brisk wind chased me through the double doors, laying out a carpet of brown leaves, blanketing the speckled marble floor with the detritus of nature. Even though the building had two perfectly functional elevators, I took the stairs out of habit to the third floor. My training had drilled into my nature a distrust of indefensible blind positions and closed-in spaces.

The room number, 359, eluded me. I strolled down several hallways, passing sequential rooms from 320 to 358, which skipped immediately to 360 a few feet away. A bundle of nerves smoldered in my gut. The meeting was set for tonight, wasn't it? It was Browning Hall, and not Renquist on the other side of campus, right? Had the professor made a typo in his email and not realized it? Maybe it was Browning 259 or even 539. On the edge of nausea, convincing myself I had already lost the job before I'd even gotten it, I made my way back down to the lobby to see if I could find a floor plan for the building when I heard a hiss behind me.

The wall opened.

Not a door. Not even a window, but a *wall.*

What had appeared to be cinderblocks coated in decades of paint cracked, and a corner intersection between the main hall and one of its offshoots proved to be hinged. My left hand went to my head, where the hilt of my silver blade sat camouflaged as a hair clip. A head full of fair hair peeked out, followed by broad shoulders covered in flannel. A moment later, the head swiveled, and I was rendered mute.

Amy would be proud of my reaction. A man with a toothy grin and dimpled cheeks complemented perfectly by deep blue eyes and blonde hair, stared at me. He was college frat boy cocky with just a touch of you-know-you-want-me male model. A perfect specimen of the type of guy my roomie would define as "the type you bed, not the type you wed." The guy oozed sex.

I shook myself from my stupor when I realized he was talking and lowered my hand, leaving the knife in its sheath, woven into my braid. "Sorry, what?"

"You don't look like a Walter, I said, but I'm pretty sure I was sent out here to find a Walter Kline."

"*Gerwalta*, actually," I corrected, holding out my hand. "Everyone calls me Geri."

Except my mother. And my father. And every hood I ever met.

"Geri," he repeated as he took my hand. *Oh, so warm. So soft. So firm. So big.* "Like the Spice Girl?"

"Except for the dancing and singing part." Deadpan, thou art mine name. "Gerwalta's old German. Just kinda hard for people to remember. Are you… Dr. Karmarov?"

Please, oh please no. But knowing my luck over the last six months, I would finally meet a guy I find attractive, and he'd turn out to be forbidden for a different reason than being a vampire.

"Me?" He ran a hand through his hair and laughed at the notion. "I'm Jess Harmond. I'm a student of Prof. Karmarov's. You're Prof. Hikimoto's student, right? The undergrad he was talking about?"

"I am. Now I remember. He mentioned there was already a graduate student on the project. Is that you?"

Grad student? I could do a grad student.

I mean, *date.* I could *date* a grad student.

"Must have been talking about me, yup. So, um, Dr. K sent me out here to get you. He's in his office at the back of the lab. Said you might have gotten lost, because he forgot to mention to you that there's a special entrance for this room. Hope you weren't wandering for too long."

"I actually was, but… No, it's okay."

Was I batting my eyelashes and giggling? Oh, my god, I was.

"But I have to admit," I continued, "even if he had told me that the door was an unmarked piece of wall, I probably wouldn't have found it any faster."

Jess looked behind him with confusion, as though he had no idea what I was talking about. When he saw the stack of pivoted bricks that was the door behind him, his mouth dropped. "How about that? Didn't know what it looked like from this side. This is an emergency exit. We never use it. This building is full of weird secrets. They even say that there was an animal lab back in the WWII days, running experiments on behalf of the government. You know those creepy towers that rise up on the corners of the building on the third and fourth floors? Doc K's lab and office are in one of those. There's an entry from the outside of the building that goes directly up here. The stuff Doc K is working on is kind of… Well, I shouldn't say anything until the two of you talk and you sign the NDA. So," he said, clapping his hands together, "let me take you, huh?"

Yes, please. Suddenly, twenty years of learned self-discipline washed down the drain. My hormones had hijacked my body and were already thinking of ways to casually ask Jess if he had a girlfriend.

Who would have guessed; I actually was female after all.

The room we entered didn't look that much different at first from any other lab in the building. Linoleum floors, off-white walls, several work areas with waist-high tables and black-cushioned stools. At the side of the room stood an emergency wash station, and next to it, a sink over which hung cartoonish signs showing proper emergency technique. No windows, however, and only four ways in or out: the door we had just come through, which looked from the inside far more commonplace and utilitarian than it had from the exterior hall, an elevator well, an arched doorway beyond which I could see a staircase spiral – I was guessing that was Prof. Karmarov's office – and a heavy brown behemoth of a door on the left wall with a large, lever-like handle.

"That's cold storage," Jess said. He must have noticed my eyes trying to figure out the details. "Restricted access, I'm afraid. Only Doc K and his staff researcher. No students allowed."

My hood hunches were piqued. "Why, what's so important about it?"

"Not important, just…" Jess winced. "Sorry, I really can't tell you until you're officially part of the team."

"Yeah, no worries." My eyes drifted up, examining an industrial ceiling dotted at intervals with what looked like an army of pen lights. "Those are some weird-looking light bulbs."

My tour guide nodded. "LEDs, actually. The lab is on an independent power grid, something about making sure that the samples in the refrigeration units stay at the right temperature even if there's a blackout. These lights don't create as much heat and are cheaper to power. Don't tell him I said so, but I think Doc K might be a secret member of Greenpeace. He has that real 'out to save the world' mentality."

"I noticed there are no windows either. I must be going crazy. I could have sworn I saw them on the outside."

"You're not crazy, there are windows," Jess said right on cue, turning an amused smile at me that made the pit of my stomach dance a jig. "Bricked over back in the '80s when this floor was used for storage. The reason Doc K fought for this space when he showed up last fall. I guess some of the samples are photosensitive."

"What, like sensitive to sunlight?"

"Yup."

He guided me towards the turret entrance. Jess opened the door and waved me on.

"Top of the stairs. I'll be here when you're done and I'll show you back down in our exclusive K-Lab elevator. Good luck, Geri."

"Thanks."

I grew dizzy as the turret crawled like a nautilus towards the tower. Memories of old castles along the windy rivers of Bavaria flooded the forefront of my mind. My annual trips to the Black Forest were for training of course, but once, when I was fourteen, my father managed to convince my mother to let me take a week-long side trip with him. We walked through medieval streets, ate chewy pretzels hot from the oven, and even went to an opera. Of course, four days in, our trip reached a dead end. A call went out for need of a hood in a nearby valley. My father was the closest and responded with haste.

I was still convinced my mother had called in a favor to make sure we didn't have *too* much fun.

At the top of the staircase, I found a door that looked more like the entry to a French cottage than a professor's office. The wooden surface, crisscrossed by iron bars with flat-nosed bolts at the intersection, would have been right at home in Lausanne or Burgundy. A wheel and lock were embedded where a plain handle may have been. I wasn't sure the professor would hear my light tapping if I tried to knock, but clueless what to do otherwise, I fisted my hand and raised it in preparation.

I'd barely made contact when the wheel spun and the door opened. The air of the room beyond, colder than that filling the staircase and the lab below, blew past me, making stray strands of my black hair fly out.

A moment later, the hair on my neck went for a similar look, and my hand flew instinctively to the hilt of the blade woven in my braid.

"Peace, Miss Kline. Peace."

The glint off the knife reflected a line of light over the vampire's forehead. I gulped, taking note of my every, numerous disadvantage. He had everything going for him: higher ground, the element of surprise, superior strength. The ability to suddenly sprout one-inch long dental daggers. The only thing I had was a two-inch blade made of a metal that wouldn't even burn him. Oh, sure, if I was lucky, I might be able to sink it in his chest and try to get halfway down the stairs, but that would be as far as I got.

"Who are you, and what did you do with Professor Karmarov?"

A gleam overcame his features, making him look boyish. He wasn't a young vamp. That is to say, when he was turned. If I had to guess, I'd put his mortal age around forty. He was far gaunter than most of his kind; a fact that may be attributable to malnourishment, or simply the roll of the genetic dice. He wasn't unpleasant to look at, but wouldn't stand out in a crowd with his curly black hair dashed in places by gray. An angular nose and a prominent chin suggested eastern European, perhaps even Russian heritage. He held his hands out before him like a cop trying to convince a kidnapper to drop his gun once cornered.

"I *am* Professor Karmarov, and I will not harm you. If you would please sheath your weapon, I can explain."

"There are no vamps at this university!" I retorted, despite the contrary evidence staring me back in the face. "It's part of the reason I came here: no supes."

"Come now, Miss Kline, as integrated as supes are in the mainstream these days, surely you don't believe there wouldn't be *any.* Though, admittedly, most vampires working in academia would think WCU too brow an institution. In my case, it is the fact that others of my kind would tend to overlook this college that led me to locating my lab and my team here."

He may have thought he was calming me, but he only made me more nervous. "Your team? So, you're not alone?"

"There are three vampires working in this lab, but I thought it would be best if you met me first, so I could orientate you to our involvement."

That's when the full implication of what he was saying hit me. "You know I'm a hood."

"Of course, I know." A tinge of smugness crept into his smile. "No need to worry. I see the fear etched into your features. I'm old enough to know the way of your kind. You're pack animals, almost as much as the wolves you counterbalance. You wouldn't be here unless it was meant to be incognito. I assure you, however, how I came to know of your nature and presence here is mere coincidence. I scented you one evening when you were working in the lab."

"Bullshit. If you had gotten close enough to smell me, I sure as hell would have picked up on your presence."

Karmarov clicked his tongue, becoming in stature every bit the professor his human cover suggested. "Firstly, you were likely scent blind at the time, given the particular concoction of sulfur dioxide you were working with. And secondly, I am a very old vampire. The reach of my senses out-performs far beyond anything a hood, no matter how mature, would be capable of. Probably beyond even that of the Red Matron."

I bit my tongue before I blabbed the fact that, as the daughter of the Red Matron, I very much doubted it.

He stepped aside and held out an arm. "Now, if you'd like to come in and discuss the matter as nothing more than a professor and a student engaging in academic exchange, I can tell you more about the project, and why, in particular, you should be interested in pursuing it."

My wordless response was to jerk my dagger a little higher.

Karmarov closed his eyes and sighed. Reaching out with dedicated ease, his hand grabbed the blade. In one clean swipe, he'd robbed me of my weapon and my self-confidence.

"If I wanted you dead, you'd be dead, Miss Kline. If I wanted a snack, between you and me, I'd opt for Jess."

A smile flitted across his face, one I found I couldn't help but share.

"Please, if you decide you don't wish to work on the project after I've had a chance to explain, I'll hold no grudge. But I think you'll find that it is in your best interest to consider otherwise."

90

TEN

"I know you're a biology student," he started once I'd settled into the chair across from him.

And by settled, I mean sat straight up, eyes forward and trained on him for the slightest implication that he would attack.

"But strictly speaking, this isn't a biology project. It isn't even an organic chem project."

"How about telling me what kind of project it *is,* then, instead of what it *isn't.*"

Karmarov ran a hand through his thinning (or thinned, I supposed, given that he no longer would age) hair. "At the moment, our work is preliminary. We're casting a wide net, not really sure which discipline is going to get us to our goal. I know as a hood, you must be very knowledgeable about wolves, but tell me —how much do you know about vampires and slayers?"

"More about your kind than slayers," I answered matter-of-factly, "seeing as slayers were never really a threat to us."

"Being that they're all extinct, I'd say they're not really much of a threat to anyone," Karmarov observed. "A vampire doesn't speak of his age in polite conversation, but suffice it to say, I'm not young, as you've probably gathered. I've been on this earth for several centuries, and I remember slayers. It was, of course, my natural inclination to dislike them, especially when I was shorter in the tooth. But through the ages, I learned that they served a very necessary and key role. Nature likes balance, and even though a species may benefit short-term from a lack of predators, in the long run, having nothing to stand in the way of its growth and dominance results in more harm than good. Are you originally from this area, Miss Kline?"

Training and a healthy dose of common sense kept my tongue still.

The professor grinned. "Forgive me, of course you have every right not to trust me with such information. Though, if I really wanted to know, as a member of the faculty, I could access your student records with just a few phone calls. I won't, of course, but please take the fact that I didn't as a token of my respect for your privacy and my professionalism in the course of this endeavor."

That fact was too true, and the understanding that he hadn't snooped relaxed my nerves. "I'm from the U.P."

"Ah, the Upper Peninsula of Michigan, yes? Well, then you may be aware of this even more so than most. Do you know what happened to the deer population in the upper Midwest when its natural predators —bears, wolves, badgers, et cetera —were hunted to near extinction during the age of the fur trappers?"

"Of course, I do," I said. Yooper school kids learned about the justification presented by thousands of Michigan deer hunters each fall in class. "The population exploded. There were so many deer that there wasn't enough food for them in winter. Not to mention how having so many of them around stunted forest growth, with them gnawing at everything that shot up out of the ground. It's part of the reason the state pushed deer hunting in the '50s and '60s. They figured it was more humane than letting thousands starve to death."

"Not to mention, venison is also very tasty." Karmarov, sitting on the edge of his desk, leaned in, sending my stomach plummeting. "Not unlike a slayer."

"Unless you're about to suggest to me that the best solution to the overpopulation of deer would have been for them to develop a sudden taste for human flesh, I'm not sure how that's relevant."

"Too true," Karmarov said as he straightened up and crossed his arms over his chest. "What I'm getting at is this. The bear, the wolves, the badgers – yes, they were predators, but they served an essential function, one that, in their absence, evolved into a much more horrific fate. As much as vampires detest slayers, they had a place in our world. In their absence this last half-century, the vampire population has begun to grow unwieldy. We've begun to fight over territory, over resources. No doubt you've heard about the increase in unsolved murders in Chicago. While some of that is merely mortal, some of the less scrupulous of our kind have taken advantage of these events to add to their clutches, including some who are not well adapted for a life of eternal, responsible imbibing of human blood."

An image of Donovan's headless corpse flashed into my mind's eye. *You're not just whistling Dixie, professor.*

He continued. "The honor code which called upon us only to use humans as donors rather than disposable prey seems to be fading into the annals of history. Huey authorities would never think to blame some of these mysterious disappearances and deaths on something as mythic as vampires, so the less morally inclined among us continue to build larger and larger families, unchecked by any limiting force. Though some of my kind may deny it, Miss Kline, we need slayers. If we do not have our balance, we will soon find ourselves stranded in the urban jungles, turning further on ourselves and our values."

"And humanity will be your forest, bitten back in the process." Fine, he had my attention, but I still wasn't clear where I fit into the picture. "So what you're trying to do is…?"

"Easy." He fanned the fingers of one hand through the air. "I'm trying to bring back slayers."

"But… they're all dead."

"I'm not so sure. You must have heard the most popular theory about their disappearance, that breeding with Hueys diminished their bloodlines."

Lectures and rants by my mother flamed the edges of memory. "Once or twice."

"Honestly, I don't know if it's true, but that some slayers did take human mates is undeniable. Though their elders frowned on the practice, it's created a wonderful opportunity for vampires like me who've realized how desperate we are for the counterbalance. You see, the slayers' DNA information has been passed down to later generations, even if dormant or recessive."

"So you're trying to extract slayer DNA?"

He nodded.

"But all the supes agreed that genetic profiling—that intentionally mapping our DNA—would be too risky. Once that information is out in the world, we can't take it back. If any wrong hands got those details, there's no telling what they might do with it."

"I'm aware of the risks. That's why this program is very small, and access to this lab, highly restricted. Besides, for the moment, I'm simply trying to identify and sequence the slayer genome. I have no intentions or plans to do that of hoods, wolves, or vampires."

"But I don't get what good having slayer DNA would be. I know there are some genetic therapies these days, but what you're talking about would be changing the physical composition of a human."

He turned sheepish, something I didn't think a vampire was capable of. "Oh, I'm not talking infection, Miss Kline. Please don't think I intend to con a score of humans into clinical trials that will lead them to become creatures of the night with glowing gold eyes and a ravenous desire for garlic. No, no. On the contrary, all around the globe, there are secret societies, ones who track all supes. Their records are long, ancient. Generation after generation of vampire, wolf, slayer, and hood bloodlines documented. I believe your people use some version of that in order to know the current whereabouts of both hoods and wolves."

"As does your kind track its own," I stated.

Karmarov nodded. "Using these records, it shouldn't be too difficult to track down some slayer descendants, perhaps even ones whose parents or grandparents were fully of that persuasion. The last known slayers only died out a few generations ago. Their mostly human descendants may have strongly related genetic sequences that, with a little tweaking, could *induce* slayerhood, for lack of a better term."

A noble cause, but one still shortsighted. "Just because you make the weapon doesn't mean it will perform well in battle. The body is only a vessel, but what would a slayer be without their traditions, their teachings? Even if you can engineer a slayer, how do you give him the ability to know how to slay?"

The professor stood, placed his hands behind his back, and began to pace. "Thus my interest in your kind."

His interest in…

My head began to shake before I even realized I was smiling. "There's no way the Matrons would agree to such a thing."

Prof. Karmarov looked down his nose at me. "Not the Matrons. I know they're too wrapped up in their power struggles and politics."

"But if not the Matrons, then wh— No, you can't be serious."

"Why couldn't I?" Amusement stretched his mouth into a grin. "Hoods, ones like you who have problems with the way your community is currently conducting itself… Surely a small cadre of such individuals could lend a hand. And in the meantime, your ability to assist in our research would be critical to success."

"How do you know I have issues with hood procedures?"

He grinned. "Would you be here, at University, on your own if not? If you had the ability to change the direction your kind – and mine – are heading, wouldn't you want to?"

I thought back to Donovan, of the gall of a baby vamp openly attacking an innocent Huey, and of his maker sending him back a few days later in a bid to kill me off. If that was the direction the vamps were heading, then Karmarov had a point.

My hesitance was all the answer he needed. "Welcome to the team, Miss Kline. Now, let's talk about your pay."

ELEVEN

Three days later, I had two big problems.

First, there was a slight chance — like, a pencil shaving's slight—that Tobias had been right. What if Donovan's maker actually did want me dead? But if that was the case, wouldn't he have sent someone else to finish what Donovan had proven to be so impotently incapable of? And if he did, wouldn't I totally die in the process? Twice I'd been challenged by a vamp — a *baby* vamp — and twice, I'd come up short and had to be saved by a werewolf.

If my cousins ever found out how pitiful I'd been in the field, I'd never live it down. Not like they would fare much better, though. I'd always been the strongest in my clan, the hood matron apparent who could kick anyone's ass — male or female — that training bouts teamed me with. As a kid, my mom had even arranged for me to spar with the Paradise alpha's son, giving me practice with an actual werewolf.

Later, I fell in love with that werewolf, and I didn't mind so much if he managed to pin me to the ground.

All my life, I'd carried silver on me — be it the two-inch blade with the embellished handle I disguised as a hair accessory woven into my braid, or bangle bracelets that I could use to shove into a wolf's maw if I got attacked. Now, I added gold to my repertoire as well. Finding 14K clip-on earrings proved a challenge, but my shopaholic roomie Amy knew how to source whatever I asked for.

"Why clip-ons?" she asked, baffled by the choice. "Your ears are pierced."

I could hardly tell her because, in the event of a vampire attack, I didn't want to tempt fate further by pulling out a traditional post earring to defend myself, thus drawing said vampire's attention to a wound gushing his favorite cocktail.

"Because of the lab," I deferred. "Some of the microbes we work with down there? Ew. I don't really want to be shoving metal through holes in my body at the end of my shift, having been exposed to who knows what."

The second problem I had wasn't so easily rationalized. I had killed a vampire. Regardless of the reasons that came about, I knew it wouldn't go without notice. Even if the maker had sent Donovan to me with the hopes I'd dispatch him, once they found out who I was, they'd take advantage of it. As my mother had told me, never waste a crisis.

When I saw my father's number flash across the screen of my smartphone, I just about had a heart attack. Truth be told, I'd been sitting on pins and needles since the moment I signed my name to the contract in Karmarov's office. Even though the professor assured me that the project, with its taboo research, was purely an academic endeavor and that no one would have any reason to know of it outside the university, I doubted something so objectionable to wolves and hoods alike would go unnoticed. The Red Matron had connections, with moles and rats from sea to shining sea, and world round.

I hit answer and launched straight into the conversation without any of the usual pleasantries. "How mad is she?"

"How *mad* is *she*?"

I bit down so hard, my tongue stung with the taste of iron. I should have known that if my mother really wanted to find a way to get me on the phone after I'd blocked her number and refused to answer her letters, she'd find a way.

"Hello, Brünhild."

"Insolent, foolish child," the Red Matron ground back with a voice that could have made nails on chalkboards sound like Mozart. "I am both your mother and your matron, and you will address me with the proper respect."

If she was giving me the choice, I'd cop to the one that didn't acknowledge the fact we were genetically linked. "Fine, *mein matrone.*"

If she picked up on the implied *fuck you* with which my tone was imbued, she didn't think it worth sidetracking. Instead, she got straight to the reason she'd finally deigned to speak to me.

"At what level does your shame manifest? How low will you sink, dragging our names along, before you come to your senses? First, you embarrass us by running away when all the family had gathered for your fire. Now, to add insult to injury, you've decided to go rogue and perform duties without edicts or justification? Your father has been worried sick over your safety as a nascent, and now we learn of this."

"Perform duties?" I didn't know exactly what part of Karmarov's research she considered part of a hood's task list. I also noticed that she didn't lump herself in on my father's side for worrying about my wellbeing. "What are you talking about?"

A gurgle on the other end preceded her airy response. "Did you or did you not kill a vampire the other night?"

A line formed between my eyes as my face screwed up. "*That's* what you're calling about? To get on my case about slaying Donovan?"

"Did you suppose I had called to coddle you?" Then, the quality of her voice shifted, becoming smaller, calculating. "Is there something else I should have called about?"

"I'd imagine the list of things I've done since leaving home that you disapprove of could fill volumes." I had long ago learned how to steer clear of the Brünhild Kline interrogation trap. "Yes, I killed a vampire the other night, but no, it had nothing to do with me acting like some righteous hood. He cornered me in an alley and told me straight up he had been ordered to kill me. I know we generally leave vampires to their own devices, but I kinda thought I was justified, seeing as it was a case of him or me. Why, whose was he? One of the people who pays you off, or someone you owe money to?"

Unfortunately, my mother likewise knew how to ignore my barbs. "Who he belongs to is of little concern to you. Now that he's dead, there's an inquiry. The crèche maker knew a hood was responsible. Figuring out it was you took little thought. How could you be so reckless?"

"*I* was the reckless one?"

"Vampires don't care for our kind," my mother spit back. "If one attacked you, you must have provoked him."

I considered waylaying into my mother about how I was sure a lot more vamps would be *craving* hood blood if they knew the healing power it seemed to have, but screw her. She could unearth that little nugget herself.

Or not. I didn't really give a fuck.

"I didn't *provoke* him. He was trying to claim my drunk roommate for his fang mitzvah, and I told him very diplomatically to get lost. Turned out, he was the kind of guy who didn't like taking no for an answer."

"You were drunk?"

To my mother, that was a worse offense than being a murderer.

"No, my roommate was drunk."

"But you were drinking too," she stated with no lack of confidence. In her book, proximity was probability, and probability, proof. "The Huey girls are a bad influence. What else are you doing? Shooting drugs and sleeping around?"

"Not that it's any of your business, but no."

Silence, then, until at last, she exhaled. "I worry."

My mother sounded like a stranger, a woman for whom genuine concern was actually possible. What game was she getting at?

"Don't be." Then, softening my own voice, I continued. "Look, I'm sorry this made its way back to you. Believe me, the last thing I want is for you to have any reason to get involved in my life. But you're the Red Matron. You're freaking Brünhild Kline. Surely the maker won't come after you for any sort of compensation. I barely defeated him as it was. If he hadn't been so young, or so cocky, he might have gotten me."

No need to mention Tobias's help in saving my skin. The last thing I wanted was for her to start asking questions about how I'd crossed paths with a lone British wolf. Or, if it was one of her plants, give her a reason to think she was successfully spying on me.

"It would… relieve your father greatly if you returned to us and performed your rites, became a fully initiated hood."

"Tell *dad* that the ability to manipulate silver and see in the dark aren't essential here. The streets are very well lit."

The alleys? Not so much.

She said nothing to that, but I swore for a moment I heard her laugh under her breath.

"I'm fine. I lead a very simple life. I go to class, I train at the gym, and I'll be starting a job soon at school. Once in a while, I go for a drink – not alcohol, in my case, anyways – with my roommate. There's nothing to be scared about."

"Parents are always scared for their children. It cannot be helped." Then, resuming her indifferent tone, she said, "The crèche maker, of course, would take grievance, even knowing his son was in the wrong. Save face, or admit to an unwise induction of a vampire who couldn't even defeat a nascent hood."

"I feel like you're trying to insult me with a great amount of stealth."

She ignored my comment, and continued. "At least there are no wolves there. I was worried some old dogs from that pack down there might come after you to get some payback, but the *oberst* reports they're all accounted for."

"Really?" I asked, an image of Tobias coming into my mind's eye. "Any from another pack, say, on vacation or passing through?"

"No, not a single one. Why?"

"Because that means you haven't sent any spies."

And with that, I ended the call.

TWELVE

Jess and I strolled across the main campus square. Midterms were fast approaching, and most of the student population had sequestered themselves to the study carrels of the library or burrowed down in their dorms. Not being a Huey gave me a slight advantage; as one of my intolerable male cousins used to say, 'We gots smarter than da Hueys.' My memory had always been sharp as well, even for a hood. Sure, I'd study, but I didn't need to become a social recluse.

Especially when the one I was being social with was so enticing.

"So hoods…" Jess started.

"Shhh!!!" I pushed a finger over my mouth before realizing there wasn't anyone nearby to overhear. Even still, I kept my voice down, and my chin curled in his direction to avoid anyone being able to read my lips. "Let's use a different word, even if it seems silly, okay?"

As soon as I'd signed the NDA, Karmarov informed me there wasn't a need to keep secrets from Jess. The Huey had been fully oriented on the particulars of his project team. Having accepted the existence of vampires, something called a hood proved quite mundane.

The adorable boy next to me grinned, but amused me. "Okay, the *Yoopers*…" he said with a wink, using the nickname Midwesterners used to refer to the people of and all things relating to Michigan's Upper Peninsula. "How are all the other kinds of – *you know* – they're all so well known, and the only real reference to your people is a single fairy tale? Everyone knows what a slayer is. Who hasn't heard of Buffy or Van Helsing?"

I quirked an eyebrow. "Who?"

"Come on, you don't know about Buf…"

"OF COURSE I know," I giggled. Yes, giggled. Which, to the untrained eye, may imply I was flirting. "Believe me, if Bram Stoker had written a book about Michel Verdun instead of Vlad the Impaler, Buffy would have worn a cape and hunted down the moon-mad." I shrugged. "I guess part of it too is because we're backwoods people. We're also not quite as, you know, extraordinary as the other… Midwesterners."

"Yeah, those Swedes, man. Fierce."

When Jess managed to bring a smile to my face, he shoulder-bumped me for good measure. Despite the fact that he was five inches taller than me and despite my having trained in hand-to-hand combat since a young age, I let myself be nudged off the path. In the back of my mind, it occurred to me that I might be flirting.

"Care to illuminate a Huey?"

"Well, as y'all are so in the dark, I suppose. What do you want to know?"

Jess motioned towards a nearby bench. We plastered ourselves in place, our bodies turned forward, but our pinkies touching. Pinkie-brushes were a good thing, right?

"First of all, what in the hell is a Huey? I hear Karmarov and his two creepy assistants say it. I mean, I know it refers to people. You know, people not from the U.P."

As a precaution, I took one more survey of our immediate surroundings. With the brick wall of the humanities building at our rear, and the whole of the interior quad nearly desolate except for a few men and one girl too far across the courtyard for me to get a good visual on. They talked amongst themselves, and not concerned with the likes of us.

"A Huey is what we call a human. Sorry, it's not really anything more exciting than that."

He pulled a pack of gum from his pocket and offered me a piece. "You shouldn't make assumptions. I can be pretty damned exciting."

Just why Karmarov had decided to bring a human in on the project was anyone's guess. Jess reported that the other two vamps that served as research assistants barely gave him the time of day, and he was an okay student, but nothing exceptional. Luckily, he'd been a night owl. In fact, Jess crossed paths with Karmarov when he pulled an all-nighter in the lab right before the fall semester finals. At 3:45 AM, the professor discovered a bright-eyed and bushy-tailed Jess in the midst of determining the mass percent composition of an aqueous hydrogen peroxide solution.

Jess leaned in, as though he were about to tell me a secret. The proximity, the smell of him, made my head swirl. The percentage of my own composition that could be described as aqueous shifted.

"So the others get all the glory and Hollywood movies, and all you guys get is a story of a little girl who wanted to go see her grandmother." He let the comment linger, and when I didn't immediately take the bait, he continued. "Any truth to it. You know, the thing about Little Red Riding Hood?"

"*Some* truth." If there was a merciful god, Jess didn't notice the way I hesitated. "The truth is very, very different from the Grimm Brothers, and definitely not something Disney would ever make a movie about."

"Tell me what really happened, then."

I looked at his gleaming white teeth, his strong chin, his total lack of facial hair and fangs, and found myself unable to resist his charms. "My people call her *Die Verräterin,* the Betrayer. She wasn't on her way to her grandmother's house; she was on her way to her clan's compound in the Black Forest. And the wolf didn't want to eat her, he wanted to…"

The words died away, and my thoughts went back in time, to me and a sweet werewolf, doing our best not to cross a line we could never come back from, but wanting to be as close to each other as possible. Cody and I discovered every technical boundary there had been around the term "virginity."

Jess tried to fill in my missing words. "I'm guessing eating her is a metaphor."

"He loved her," I let out in a huff. "And she loved him. They married in secret, in a Huey village where none were the wiser of their natures. They were happy for a short time, our history says. But there're downsides to being a wolf. They're pack animals; their whole psychosis demands that they remain with a pack. The wolf who loved *Die Verräterin* left his pack to be with her. After a little time, he began to bear the burden of his separation. We call it lunacity."

"Hueys know all about lunacy," Jess supplanted. "You've seen how politics works in Chicago, haven't you?"

A smile ghosted across my face. "No, not lunacy, *lunacity.* After three moon cycles, a lone wolf loses his humanity. He becomes the wolf for good. As Little Red's wolf husband veered toward lunacity, the Matron of her bloodline performed her sacred duty. She killed the wolf."

Jess's jaw went slack. "That's one badass mother-in-law."

I nodded.

"So, then what?" he asked, scooting closer to me, the anticipation roiling in his eyes. "No cross-dressing werewolves or huntsman hacking people out of his stomach."

"I've always supposed the wolf dressing in the grandmother's clothing was a metaphor. You know, like a power play, him showing the matron that he could steal her daughter away and control her. I don't know, I'm not really sure where that bit of the fairy tale comes from."

"And the ax?" Jess said.

I swallowed down my nerves. "There was an ax. They used it to cut the baby out of *Die Verräterin*. Then they used it to cut her and the baby into tiny pieces. The Red Matron roasted all three of them like kebabs on silver spits over a sacred fire."

I didn't know why the truth of it should bother me. Still, I found my head hanging low. A moment later, the sorrow flew away, warmed beyond comfort by the feeling of Jess's hand underneath my chin. I looked up, and felt my lungs seize up when the intensity of his concerned gaze met mine.

"I'm sorry."

I licked lips that had gone suddenly dry. "There's nothing for you to be sorry about."

"Of course there is. I asked you to tell the story. If I knew it was so painful for you, I wouldn't have. Tell you what."

As quickly as the heat had started to fill my fingers and dance in the pit of my stomach, Jess was on his feet, leaving me bereft.

He reached for me. "Let's get a cup of coffee and talk about silly things, like the campus football team and how stupid Dean Whitmore is for wearing a toupee in a city famous for its wind."

"Coffee and mockery? It's like bingo night."

THIRTEEN

My body pulsed as I gripped the nearly frozen metal handle to the equally prosaic metal door, the private entrance for Karmarov's lab. As though a piece of ice had been slipped beneath my skin, the frigid sensation shot up the network of nerves, over my wrists, and up to my shoulders. Inside the door, things didn't get much better. As I used the plastic ID I'd been given to call the elevator, the hairs on the back of my neck rose to attention. By the time the door opened, I practically fell into it, and into Jess in the process.

His awkward smile and curious gaze held me in place as I stared at him, wearing the sloppy gooey face of a doe-eyed girl. "Are you okay?"

"What, me?" I finally managed to blink and waved my hand in the air. "Fine, it's just… The full moon sort of throws my senses off."

Throws them into hyperdrive, was more accurate.

To my surprise, when I looked up from the floor and met Jess's eyes, he was beaming.

"What?"

Jess leaned forward, his forehead touching mine as his free hand worked to angle my chin up. "You're all flushed and… Sorry, it's inappropriate."

"No, that's fine. Be inappropriate. What were you going to say?"

No time for the warm wash of liquid goo over me; the door into the lab opened at just that second. Whatever he'd been on the verge of melting me with would have to wait.

I still remembered my first day of work at the state park. I had heard the term "butterflies in your stomach" as a child, but I didn't think it accurately captured the semi-toxic feeling, as though someone had poured acid down my throat so that it could slowly eat away my insides. In that case, I'd known most of the people I'd be working with at the state park. The head ranger, Rick Ryland, had been my boyfriend's uncle, and the only wolf whom my mother had ever admitted to once considering "not a total wretch."

If that day had felt like acid eating my innards, then today, I felt like I'd done a double shot of liquid hot magma with a nuclear fusion chaser. Some things proved similar, however. My boss? Not a werewolf, but a vampire. My mother? Unsupportive. (Or, at least, I knew she would be if she ever found out.) My uniform? Unflattering. I supposed it was only appropriate to wear a lab coat, working in a lab. But as I'd decided that flirting with Jess wouldn't be totally objectionable, I wished it came in a more form-hugging fit and, if possible, in red.

Karmarov grinned at me. "Ready to meet the rest of the team, Miss Kline?"

Before I could follow up, a light tap on my shoulder sent my instincts flaring. Within a heartbeat, I had my petite dagger before me, and Jess pushed protectively behind me.

Amused, and not in the least bit frightened, three vampires wore saccharine grins as they looked at me in my defensive pose, ready to protect a human with nothing but my cunning and a two-inch silver blade. If I'd been a Huey who didn't know any better, I'd have said the two new faces belonged to fellow college students. That is, that they were college aged. The girl I'd place in her early twenties at the time of her turning, and the guy, just a few years younger. How old they really were was anyone's guess. Like most of their kind, they possessed the tempered duality of being completely nondescript and, if you let your eyes fall on them and observe at length, beautiful in a way that defied logic. Despite the fact that both she and he appeared to be Asian, their pallor drew the eye, almost as if they'd covered themselves in some sort of iridescent powder. Her green eyes and his brown ones tracked me as I strove to drive down my instincts and walk step by labored step off the elevator and into the lab proper.

Karmarov assumed his best detached scientist voice to the others. "As I mentioned before, hoods don't experience quite the rabid surrender to animal nature that a wolf does leading up to a full moon, but it's not uncommon for them to have some mild symptoms. It's very fascinating, really. I suspect something at the genetic level, of course. Miss Kline, you can lower your weapon. Neither Kai nor Cynthia are going to harm you.

Remember that I discussed this with you, that there were two more vampires working on the project?"

Did he? Looking back in the memories of our conversation, I supposed that he had. Still…

I looked back over my shoulder to Jess, and saw no panic or worry at all. He winked at me, then jerked his chin in the trio's direction.

"They're perfectly harmless."

The female vamp huffed and planted a fisted hand on her hip. "I beg to differ." Then, as if she'd never heard Jess's unintentional insult, she took on the repose of a Walmart greeter, holding out her icy hand. "Hi, I'm Cynthia Wu. I just started my third PhD, this one in bioengineering."

My head slowly dipped. "Your… third?"

"I already have doctorates in PoliSci and Asian History. That second one's a personal passion, of course."

"Of course." I turned to the young male vampire. Like Cynthia, he had the same Far Eastern complexion, but something in his manner seemed much more… western.

"Kai," he said, jerking his head as though he'd just broken the surface of the ocean and was ridding his brow of it.

"Hawaiian?"

His smile went from bubbly to 100-watt. "Oh, you recognize the name. Yeah, totally. Gnarly."

Karmarov, who had been circling in observation, dipped in closer to where we all stood. "You have to forgive Kai's out-of-date expressions. He was turned in the late '80s and I'm afraid he's never let go the vernacular. It's like working with Spicoli."

If Karmarov meant to insult Kai, it fell flat. Instead, the Pacifica vampire beamed. "Totally. The character was *awesome*."

"No, it's just…" I stumbled verbally, looking in my memories for long ago lessons on the decorum of polite vampire society. "I didn't know there were vampires in Hawaii. Doesn't seem a very welcoming environment. There are certainly no werewolves there."

Karmarov grinned. "Which enhances its appeal for a vampire. Why don't you three get to work while I give Miss Kline a quick orientation?"

Without a word, the others turned to their respective tables and did as instructed. Karmarov flicked his fingers, motioning me towards an unattended table at the far side of the lab.

"Do you remember those secret societies I told you about? The ones that track the goings-on of all supernatural creatures?"

"Of course."

Karmarov continued. "You may be interested to know there is no mention of either slayers nor hoods in their most ancient annals."

"But the hood archives go way back to Biblical times."

He shook off what turned out to be evidence of my ignorance. "Vampires can trace our ancestry as far back as Nineveh, and the wolves, to the building of the Sphinx."

"So there's some truth to the Anubis and Lilith lineage myth?"

This time I had Karmarov at a disadvantage. "Is that something taught in the hood bloodlines?"

I nodded. "We're told the first werewolf and the first vampire were the results of ancient kings breeding with gods. Used that story once or twice to argue myself out of bible school when I was little." *What's with all the one and only god, then,* I'd say, to the point of driving my mother to the end of her wits.

The professor bared his teeth – sans fangs, I noticed – at my quip. "And what origin story do you have for your own existence?"

I searched the cobwebs of memory. "I don't know that we have one."

His finger went up as if to say *eureka!* "Because you were *engineered.* Hoods and slayers both were; that's my theory, anyway. My goal – our goal – is to figure out how, and do it again. In this lab…" His hand ghosted the air at our surroundings. "…we begin that task. Through my contacts around the world, I have amassed genetic samples from all the slayer lines, some as old as the sixteenth century. We will catalog them, work the bloodlines backward, and see if we can't figure out what it was that caused the mutation to begin with."

He reached under the table and pulled out a box of one-inch long glass slides.

"Each table has its own sequencer. What you and Jess will be working on is feeding the slides, one by one, running the analysis, and examining the computer's report for any noted anomalies or uniqueness. It's somewhat tedious, and I'll admit, boring work, but a necessary step for the project to move forward."

Having never worked on anything in a lab dealing with genetics, I found my curiosity piqued. I pulled the tray of glass slides in my direction and picked up the one in the furthest corner, holding it up to the light to examine it. "If slayers went extinct half a century ago, how did you manage to get DNA samples?"

If a vampire was capable of blushing, Karmarov would have. "Unlike vampires, slayer bodies do not burn to ash when exposed to sunlight. In fact, they hold up very nicely."

Realizing the implications, and with my mind's eye suddenly filled with the image of two men in beaten-up clothes tunneling into a slayer grave and heaving out the body, I almost dropped the slide. The look on my face must have tipped off the professor to my conclusion.

"Oh, no, nothing covert, I can assure you. We received permission in most cases from surviving family to excavate. There were only a few gravesites which required less-than-legal-or-ethical attention. Now," he said, looking at his watch, a platinum-plated trinket I was willing to bet cost more than my rent. "I have a teleconference I'm supposed to be joining in a few minutes, and I need time to review my notes. Ask Jess to show you the ropes of working the machine and how to read the results. Oh, and Miss Kline?"

"Yes?"

"If the moon always has such a strong effect on you, you might be wary of taking the elevator up in Mr. Harmond's company when it's near full. I may have brought you in on this project due to your chemistry, but not necessarily the part of it between you and Jess."

"I wasn't… We weren't…"

His finger in the air cut me off. "I know. But let's just say, you both were a little flush."

FOURTEEN

Victor Clements had massive hands. I knew this both from my roommate's reports, and because he emerged from the kitchen of the frat house holding three beer bottles in only one palm.

I clicked my tongue when he offered. "No thanks."

That smile defined sly and sexy. No wonder Amy had fallen for him in the span of a week. He was just the right combination of hot and ill-advised to meet her profile. "Nobody's going to card you here, Geri. You don't have to be such a goody-two-shoes."

"Geri doesn't drink," Amy informed him, taking the bottle her new beau offered and twisting off the top.

Propping himself up next to Amy against the wall, Victor laughed. "What's the point of coming to an Alpha Beta Delta party if you're not planning on getting wasted?"

Before I even had a chance to rise to my own defense, Amy did so for me.

"Amy doesn't drink, Vick. Not can't, or shouldn't. *Doesn't.* Is that going to be a problem, because if this place is only for bingeing, and doesn't know how to show everyone a good time, your frat is kinda lame."

My eyes blinked rapidly as I tried to rationalize this new Amy. Too bad she couldn't be so respective of my lack of love life.

"Thanks, Amy. Victor, like she said, it's just not for me."

Any concern he might have feigned fell away with a shrug. "Whatever. Come on, Amy." He pulled at my roommate's sleeve. "You said you're a physics major. I want you to show me all about getting physical."

And like that, they were gone, the bouncing, mingling crowd swallowing them as they drifted away. I looked around me, hoping that Jess had turned up. I'd texted him as soon as Amy had convinced me to go out tonight. He texted back that he was studying, but he'd try to swing by.

As I wandered into what was probably a dining room under normal circumstances, a flash of pale flesh caught the corner of my eye. The vampire somehow managed to blend into the crowd, and seem to not be a part of it at the same time. He'd been frozen at just the right age to fit the crowd; I'd place him in his early twenties when he'd been turned. Whenever that was had been an era when men wore their hair shoulder-length. His blond locks and flannel reminded me of Kurt Cobain. That he'd been waiting for me to look in his direction couldn't be disputed; the moment our eyes met, he jerked his head to the side, motioning for me to follow.

Normally, you'd tell a child of the night to go screw himself if he tried to get you alone. Me? I'd been almost killed by one of the bastards not too long ago, and I still needed answers as to why. The vamps in my lab were no good. They had all arrived in Chicago too recently to have a grasp on what the local clutches were up to.

If I was going to get to the bottom of this, I'd have to do it on my own.

Even outside, despite the fact that the late March air was still pretty nippy, a half-dozen couples sat in armchairs or curled up on blankets on the humble front lawn. The vamp sauntered us past them, not even turning to look at me. When we got far enough away from the frat house for the sounds of the voices within to begin to fade, I stopped.

"If you think you're going to lure me to an alley, know that I'm not going to fall for the same trick twice."

He pivoted with the speed of a sloth. "This will work then. Come closer."

"Nope, I'm good here. If you got something to say to me, say it."

He hesitated a moment, before making his pronouncement in his flat baritone. "Leave Chicago or suffer the consequences."

"Really, that's what you're going to try to pull? Guess what? Every badly written horror movie from the past thirty years called. They want their clichés back."

"If you stay, we will not be held responsible for the consequences. Not the ones for you. Not the ones for your family."

My ire fired within. "My family has nothing to do with my being here."

"That's what you think. Decide what you will. You have been warned." His eyes rolled as he turned and began to stalk up the street. Following him with my gaze, I caught sight of someone I actually wanted to see.

Jess rounded the corner at the end of the block just as Vampire Kurt turned around it. He caught sight of me and waved, picking up the pace to reach me.

"Was that a vamp?"

My hands flew up, and I shot him a warning expression. "Hueys."

"Oh, right." His brow furrowed as he considered alternatives. "Was that a… Swede?"

"Yes, Jess, that was most definitely a Swede. Maybe even a Viking."

Given his appearance, it wasn't impossible.

"What did he want?"

"What do all Swedes want? To be creepy Swedes and act all Swedish. I'm glad you made it, Jess, but I have to tell you, I don't really want to go back in there, if you don't mind."

"Fine by me. I was only coming to spend some time with you anyway. Still, it's a beautiful night. Would be a shame to waste it. What do you want to do?"

The night air filled my lungs as I pulled in a deep breath. The waning moon above still managed to keep the night sky bright. It would be the kind of moon back home that would have lit up the woods when Cody and I would sneak out to meet each other. Not for the first time, I wondered if my ex-boyfriend was even capable of the kind of wistful nostalgia I felt at times like these, or if being mated blocked him from remembering how in love we'd been once upon a time.

Jess snapped inches from my face. "Hello, Geri, you there? You wandered off for a moment."

I smiled my apologies. I might not still have Cody, but Jess was here and waiting.

"You up for a walk?" I asked.

He offered out his arm. "With you? I'd be delighted."

With no real destination, we meandered the edge of campus for an hour, talking about the useless miasma that passed for conversation in the early stages of a relationship. When he laughed at a joke I made, it felt like magic.

Jess motioned to a nearby bench as we passed through one of the college's courtyards. The three-quarters moon rose overhead, lacing my insides with temptation. I never thought I'd miss running through the woods at night. My soul, my body, ached for it. I crossed my arms over my chest, hugging myself, tempering my breath.

"You're doing it again."

One eyebrow angled precipitously as I looked to Jess.

"Acting like you're modeling a straightjacket," he continued. "Am I making you crazy?"

"What? No!" Immediately, my arms and hands lashed out, and I tried to look as non-bundled as possible. "It's just, the moon. It does things to me. It… Oh, jeez, I guess when I say things like that, it does sound crazy, doesn't it?"

Jess slid closer, dripping an arm over the back of the bench behind me. His voice took on a secretive hush, even though there wasn't anyone nearby. "Is it a hood thing?"

"I don't know. I think?" Sitting back, I was thrilled to discover he didn't shy away —or worse, push me— when

I leaned my head into his shoulder. "It's kind of like lunar separation anxiety. Ever since I left my clan last fall, I'm uncomfortable in my own skin sometimes. My instincts get stir-crazy."

"That doesn't surprise me," Jess said. "Christmas is just a tradition, but people who are separated from their families can actually become ill from it. You're a strong woman, enduring something like that month after month."

I'm weaker by the day, I wanted to say, but was afraid to admit even to myself that it was true. Every moon that came and went, I felt the urgency to act build inside of me. Running myself ragged and going through forms at the gym took some of the edge off, but even Amy had noticed how my "inner bitch had a regular stopover," joking that she'd never seen a PMS case as severe as mine. Every full moon that passed left residual effects, a hangover that grew longer with each cycle.

Shivers broke me from my inner machinations when the arm Jess had been resting on the back of the bench hooked around, and he ran lazy fingers down my cheek.

"Anything I can do to help?"

I shook my head. "I get through it. But, damn, if it wouldn't cause so much drama, I'd love to dance around the bonfires at *feuernacht* just one more time."

From beyond my view, Jess's other hand circled around. My eyes focused on his balled-up fist, of his fingers wrapped around a lighter. With a flick and a scratch, a petite flame burst from it, dancing, winking at me.

My head rotated, looking up into his grinning face.

"It's not quite a bonfire," he said, "but if it helps, I'll dance around it with you."

And then, I kissed him.

My lips moved over his tenderly at first, disorientating, gauging his acceptance. Within moments, my excitement had turned to panic. Oh my god, what if he thought I was a bad kisser? What if I *was* a bad kisser? Did I have bad breath? What was the last thing I ate? Tuna fish? Had it been tuna fish? How in the hell did I let myself eat tuna fish on the day that I was going to kiss Jess Harmond for the first time? Was it also going to be the last time? Was he going to curl up his nose in disgust and say it had been a mistake? What if I never kissed another boy again? What if, as Amy warned, I died a virgin?

"Geri?"

One eye opened, ready to see him rolling his tongue like he'd just licked a toad. "Yeah?"

He met my gaze with a smolder that shut down all thought and turned on my whole body. "You don't have to think so much about it. Just kiss me."

His wish was my command. I leaned in and pressed my mouth to his again, this time relaxing into his body. Jess's hand moved from my cheek, up the side of my face, over my ear, until he threaded his hand through my hair and angled my head. The position allowed him to deepen the kiss as his tongue entered my mouth. Before I realized what I was doing, my own hands had circled his neck to pull myself toward him.

It all came crashing down when something punched me in the gut.

I gasped and pulled away from Jess, getting to my feet, my hands pushing into my stomach, trying to push down the spasm.

"Geri?" Concern watered Jess's eyes. "What's wrong?"

"Wolf."

My answer ground out of my throat, an echo of the psychic energy the nearby beast was dishing out. Hoods sensed wolves, of course, but I also had a bit of psychic empathy where they were concerned. Call it animal instinct. Even if a zebra didn't see the lion, instinct told it when it was being stalked. Somewhere nearby, there was a wolf, and he was throwing out serious negative and hostile vibes in my direction.

Jess's head spun, surveying the square. "Where?"

"Close. A few hundred yards, maybe. Jess, go. I need to find…"

But I didn't need to find him. A moment later, when I forced myself erect and went into hunting mode, as if by instinct, my eyes found his.

FIFTEEN

Upper lip curling, teeth bared, Tobias glared at me like a madman threatening death and promising pain. Had he been any closer, I would have heard his growl. Even across the square, I could see those eerily white canines of his grow long and wanton. He wanted to destroy me. He wanted to rip me, limb from limb.

A wave of desire soaked through me. I wanted it more. I wanted *his blood.*

"If you got something to say to me, come say it."

No sooner had I called him out than he turned to run. I was in pursuit without thinking. Jess's voice grew small as my steps grew quicker. Even with the taste of him still on my tongue, I couldn't suppress my predisposition. I had become a huntress, inverting Tobias's nature and intentions, making the prey into the predator.

A werewolf's propensity to run in his animal form would have left me behind in the dust, but as bipeds, a hood held favor. Tobias cut through a crowd of students holding a demonstration in an archway. A woman, knocked aside, screamed obscenities which faded as I too passed her. At the edge of campus, he managed to slip out of view, but he wasn't safe yet. There was no doubt in my mind which way he went. Even from two blocks away, I could hear the rush of water and the clacking branches of leafless trees blown in the night wind inside of LaBagh Woods.

I pushed my body, striving, straining, needing to reach him. If he got more than a few hundred feet into those woods, out of sight from the main paths, he'd shift into his wolf and I'd lose him for sure.

Ground made paste by the barely-above-freezing temperatures and rain of the previous day rendered every footfall a struggle. Luckily, that was true for Tobias as well. I heard his grunt only moments before I saw him. Trying to shake his feet free of the muck, he was already peeling off clothing, revealing a bare chest glazed by a sheen of mist from the damp night air. His hands worked at his belt. Despite the burning in my muscles telling me I was going to pay for this tomorrow, I did what I must. I leapt, tackling him to the ground.

Tobias collapsed, kissing dirt. "Get off me, hood!"

"Not until you tell me why you're spying on me!" I shouted, wrestling his belt from his hips and using it to bind his wrists behind his back.

"I'm not. Ow!" All attempts to bring his arms back around front failed. "Are you one of those Americans raised on a pig farm?"

"Better, I was raised a Yooper."

"A *whaaat*?" His face screwed up as he looked back at me over his shoulder. "What the Dickens is a Yooper?"

"Me." Shifting my hips, I was able to plant a knee between his shoulder blades as my hand filled with his shoulder-length, greasy brown hair. "Why are you following me?"

"For the last bloody time, my being here has nothing to do with you. My God, are all American hoods this paranoid, or are you special?"

"Am I supposed to believe you just happened to show up *again* by chance? And what was that growly thing back there? Are you seriously going all territorial? Oh my god, are you following me around because you have some sort of crush on me? You got jealous when you saw me kissing another boy?"

Tobias let his forehead fall into the mud as I released my grip. "No, you're definitely special. Look, Gerwalta, I swear to you on the haunches of my alpha and father, I don't give a bullfrog's left bullock who you go around kissing. But three times since I came to Chicago I've been on the scent of who I came here to find, and all three times, following that scent led me to you. I'm starting to think you're the one sleeping with the enemy."

"Ha! Shows what you know. I'm not sleeping with anyone."

"Can't imagine why." He shook with silent laughter. "Please get off me. If I have to throw you off, you're going to get hurt."

"Excuse me, but which of us is the badass who just ran down a werewolf and tackled him to the ground?"

"I let you tackle me. Have to admit, your sudden resurgence of BDSM threw me for a loop."

"For the last time, I am *not* into sadomasochism!" I declared and threw my hands up in the air.

Which, it turned out, was a mistake.

The moment I withdrew the pressure of my knee between his shoulder blades, Tobias rolled to the side with such force, I was thrown to the ground beside him. Despite having both his hands behind his back, he moved with lupine grace and speed. His weight atop me rendered my ability to sit up, let alone stand, impossible. Tobias covered my body with his own, his legs straddling me at the hip, making the ability to kick him impossible.

His canines, still extended, skimmed the sensitive skin at the base of my ear, sending shivers through my body.

"One bite, hood," his gravelly voice teased as he spoke into my ear. The feel of his warm breath triggered a gasp, but I wasn't entirely sure it was from fear. Instead, another more feral sensation was boiling my blood. "One bite, and I could end you."

"If you don't want anyone to know you're here, I'd suggest not killing the only daughter of the Red Matron."

He pulled, wide-eyed. "The Red… You're the Red Matron's daughter?"

A smile ghosted my lips, seeing him at a disadvantage. "The *only* daughter. In fact, the only *child.* The only hope for her illustrious line to continue. So while I'm not really into being dead right now, at least I'd go with the knowledge that you'd be joining me after a most painful and dishonorable death."

He changed strategy, whispering against my lips instead as his smoldering eyes looked right into mine. "Maybe instead of kill you, I'll simply take you. We all know what happens to hoods who lay with a wolf, don't we? And you've already been branded with *Die Verräterin*'s name, so all I'd be doing is helping you fulfill your destiny. What would your Red Matron mother think then?"

I tried to deny corrupt impulses firing on full throttle. God, his body on mine felt so good. A pull in the pit of my stomach was sending commands to my limbs, demanding that they get with the program, reach out to touch him. I became uber aware of his domination, how without even his own hands to assist him, he had me at his complete mercy.

And blood of my ancestors help me, I liked it.

But a lifetime of training wouldn't so quickly lapse. An expert in disguising my inner emotions with a war mask, I kept my expression and my movements under command. I gave Tobias nothing he could interpret as weak or manipulated.

"You'd honestly doom yourself to a lifetime of being bonded to me sexually just to piss off my mother?"

"If I am unable to complete the mission I'm here for because of your interference, my life has no other purpose than revenge." He leaned in, sniffing me, running his tongue over the throbbing vein in my neck. "You think I can't scent your arousal, hood? If I tried to take you right here and right now, you wouldn't say no."

I gave him a flash of a toothy grin. "No, I wouldn't." Then, putting all my strength into breaking my right leg free and thrusting it up, I slammed my knee into the big dipper extending down from his full moon. "I'd say *hell* no."

Tobias rolled off me, howling, whimpering, folding himself into a fetal position. I rose to my feet, doing my best to push the muck and leaves off my clothing. He'd be fine in a few minutes, which I hoped was long enough to get the hell away.

SIXTEEN

I'd sensed his proximity for the better part of five minutes when he finally found his backbone and the door to the diner. Tobias plopped down in the booth across the table from me and glared. Glared like a professional Olympic badminton judge, complete with all the, you know, world-class judgey-ness.

"Tobias."

I didn't bother looking up from my *Introduction to Genetics* text. "Stop by so you could threaten to seduce me again, or just happen to be looking for a bite? If the latter, I'd try the lamb. I hear they serve it extra raw here."

He ran a hand through his hair, which, like his clothes and his personality, could do with some serious scrubbing.

"I'msorryaboutsayingthosethingstoyou."

His mumbled frankenword failed to communicate much of anything, but when I looked up at his crestfallen expression, I could tell that it was taking every ounce of remorse for him to get it out.

"What was that?"

"I said, I'm sorry about what I said the other night," he said through gritted teeth. "I shouldn't have implied I could smell your… You know what. It was ungentlemanly, and I apologize."

I closed the book and hitched my chin on a balled fist. "Rare are the occasions when a werewolf is mistaken for a gentleman. However, I'm now positive you're not faking the whole being British thing."

"I'm English, not British. And you're a hood. Most of your kind wouldn't give me the benefit of a doubt when it comes to being human."

"I hear that's often true of the English. Then again, my father is Argentinian, so I may have inherited his biases."

Rather than be offended by my remarks, he dismissed them with a sigh. "I mean, most hoods wouldn't look for my humanity. They'd only see the wolf, the monster, the thing they must beat into submission, dominate, destroy. But you're not like most hoods I've met."

"Two days ago, I chased your ass into the forest, knocked you to the ground, and threatened to gut you," I said. "This is what you consider an improvement?"

"It's better than most of my encounters with hoods back home. But even if you had treated me like that from the beginning, I have to pay up my own fines. Calling you out on what was more than likely a purely subconscious physical response was beneath me." The corners of his mouth twitched. "No pun intended."

I took a long sip of my coffee, fixing him in my gaze, before responding. "You wouldn't be the first wolf who propositioned me."

His face screwed up. "But why would a wolf want to sleep with *you*?"

The way he said *you*, the tone with which he slanted the word, could have been replaced with *the severed head of a camel* or *Charlie Sheen* with the same level of disgust. Glaring, I crossed my arms over my chest and shot a medieval treasure trove of daggers his way.

Tobias, ashen-faced, scrambled to correct himself. "I don't mean *you,* like ew, who would want that? I mean you, who is not only definitely not a wolf, but also a hood?" He leaned in over the table, dropping his voice. "Wolves mate for life, without exception. You'd think someone like you would know that."

It amused me that, of all the things we had said, that was the thing he thought needed to be protected from stray ears. "We were both aware of that. He was willing, I was not. And for your information, we *had* been dating for the better part of two years."

"*You* dated a lycanthrope?" Tobias asked, incredulous. "You, the daughter of the Red Matron?"

"The fact that it pissed off my mom made it all the more enjoyable. In fact she..." I cut myself off. *That,* frankly, was none of his business. I threw up my hands in frustration. "Look, I'm from a tiny town with only five hundred people in it. Pickings were slim. So, yes, if you want to know why I treat werewolves with general acceptance, that's part of it. If you also want to know why I have trust issues with particularly good-looking male werewolves about my own age, I'd see Part A of this statement."

The unintended flirtation was out of my mouth before I realized it. My cheeks burned red, and Tobias took no aims to hide his amusement. Luckily, proving that he was (usually) a gentleman, he continued as if I said nothing.

"Are we good then?"

He extended a hand across the table. A hand that shook even as it waited for mine to join it. Why? Was he stressed? Was he nervous? Was he…

I narrowed my gaze, noticing what at first had escaped my attention. The shine of his eyes had faded. His hair, beyond oily, was now both matted and full of dirt. His clothes hadn't been quite so threaded at the edges last I saw him. Under his eyes, dark, puffy pockets that would have set any doting mother into a tizzy.

I sat up as his hand dropped away slowly. "How long has it been now?"

His eyes darted away, as if he'd been caught in the midst of a lie. He crossed his right arm over his body and rubbed his opposite forearm. I didn't need to specify what I was asking about; it was obvious to both of us what banner the elephant in the room wore.

"Two full moons. I left my pack right after the wane."

Dear god, no wonder he looked such a wreck. "Are you insane? What are you doing lingering around Chicago? Even the strongest wolves can't get through a third full moon without going loony. As young and as far away from your territory as you are, I'm surprised you got through two without doing something horrific to some innocent Huey."

"I was able to lock myself up the last full moon," he said, running a hand over his face. "No one was injured, but it took everything I had just to come back to two legs."

"I don't get it. What is it that's going on in Chicago that has you so determined to stay even though one more month is going to leave you trapped in your wolf form for the rest of your life? Go home!"

Don't put me in a situation where I have to be the one to kill you.

"Do you remember the night we met, Geri?"

The sudden shift in subject gave me whiplash. "What?"

"When you and your drunk friend got cornered by the vamp behind the pub?"

"One, my friend has a name, which you know is Amy. Two, in America, they're called *bars,* not *pubs.* And three, as I told you before, I would have been able to handle it just fine if you hadn't come along."

A silver streak passed through his eyes. "He literally had your passed-out friend stashed in a pile of rubbish and you, dangling off the ground as he tried to choke you to death."

"All part of my plan," I bluffed.

Tobias paused a moment, as though deciding if it was worth it to reopen the debate. "Whatever. My point is: it wasn't coincidence that I was passing by. I had been tracking that vampire all night. He'd had a few other scores lined up that he gave up on when he noticed me tailing him. He probably guessed, and correctly, that I might follow him back to the crèche."

"What possible interest would a wolf have in a baby vamp breeding house located halfway around the world?"

Then, as though I was on a gameshow where a leggy, blonde assistant had just turned over a sign with the obvious answer to the grand prize jackpot question, it all snapped into place.

My throat tightened. "If you're a few weeks away from lunacity, your only hope is to go back to your own pack or find a way to join another. Why don't you?"

"Because I can't. I've been exiled."

SEVENTEEN

My grandmother had told me once when I was a child that magic made werewolves animals, but their sense of community and family gave them their humanity. Without the latter, only the former remained. Eventually, a lone wolf, deprived those connections, would lose his human form. As supernaturally strong predators who didn't fear humans, they'd be a danger to themselves, and everyone around them.

That's when a hood would step in. Asking a packmate to destroy one of his own was an indelible cruelty, almost like asking a mother to slaughter her own child. Hoods had no qualms terminating a wolf gone permanently moon-mad. We killed on sight, and slept like babies. At least, most hoods did.

I was not most hoods. In the space of a few seconds, my mind's eye filled with images of Tobias's wolf form, headless, his blood staining my hands. Fear struck me —not just because I worried for his safety, but because that vision filled me with a carnal pull, a bloodlust I had rarely known.

When I could find the ability to form words again, my voice was high and airy. "You're a rogue?"

"Not by choice," he said. "Don't think I don't know what's coming if I can't amend this soon. I'm running out of time."

"That's kinda my point. I mean, look at yourself. You look like a junkie, like a meth head. Do whatever it takes, Tobias. Beg, barter, get them to take you back."

"They won't," he insisted with a huff. "Not unless I come back with proof, not unless I can show them evidence."

"Evidence of what?"

A grey cloud drifted in over his already gaunt features. His jaw tightened as his teeth ground. Then, with a huff only a broad-chested wolf could make, both his body and his tongue relaxed.

"My pack is based in rural England, up in the north. A few years ago, a vampire clutch moved near our territory, but we didn't care. How would it affect us? They were in town, we lived out in the countryside. Soon, a dead body turned up in the river, then another a week later in a parking lot. Then, a few more. Nothing in numbers unusual for a city the size of Morpeth, and always people who didn't have much in the way of friends or family. It was obvious to me, however, that the deaths bore the common markers of a baby vamp losing control. All happened a few hours before dawn, all without signs of a violent struggle or forced entry, all missing sizable amounts of blood. Still, we didn't think it was our business. Until one of our own became a victim."

I couldn't catch the air before I sucked in a gulp. "But I thought vampires only preyed on humans."

"Me, too. But the Morpeth clutch— it was almost as if they were field scientists, collecting data. They keep logs, write out notes, have a lab where they run experiments."

My eyebrow arched. "How do you know?"

A grim but boastful cock in his smile preceded Tobias's answer. "Because I broke into their compound. During the day, while they slept. The wolf they killed? It wasn't just any wolf, it was my brother."

"What!?" I reached out across the table on instinct, covering Tobias's hand with my own. As expected, the chill I normally got until I'd acclimated to a wolf ran up my spine.

"I'm so… I'm so sorry." Then, *trying* to maintain some proper indifference, I circled back. "But if you knew the vamps were responsible for killing your brother, didn't your alpha see that as justified? Hell, if one of your pack had been murdered, wouldn't that even be his responsibility?"

"It should have been," he agreed, "if it hadn't been the alpha who was murdered."

A double whammy, where pack dynamics and Tobias were concerned. Not only had he lost a sibling, his pack had lost their leader.

"The new alpha refused to listen to me, insisted I was seeing boogiemen in broom closets. Even after I showed him a few of the documents I'd taken. He just took them from me and threw them in the fireplace. Eventually, the clutch ferreted out that I was the one who broke in. They demanded an explanation, compensation. Our alpha rolled over, told them he'd do anything they wanted to keep the peace between our peoples. They wanted me exiled."

"To kill you themselves would have started a blood debt," I said aloud at the realization. "Your offense wasn't enough to ask for your death, but they still wanted you dead. To kill you themselves wasn't going to work, but by having you exiled, they pretty much guaranteed the same result. As a rogue, eventually you'd go mad, and a hood would be forced to end you. But I still don't see how that leads you here?"

Tobias shook his head. "There's another wolf pack just slightly south of us. Two days after my brother died, their beta went missing. I found her name listed on one of their charts, and with a note saying that she would be sent off to Chicago."

"And what makes you think that meant this part of Chicago? It's a huge city."

The dismissiveness evident in my tone made Tobias's words sharp.

"My instincts drew me to this side of town. I caught her scent a few blocks from campus when I first got here. That would have been two days after Kara disappeared. More than three days, and the trail would have faded too much for me to pick up. I've been keeping my eyes open for vampires in this area since then. That vamp who attacked you was the first I'd found in the area since I'd arrived."

"Did you follow him back to his crèche? Poke your nose around there?"

Tobias shook his head. "Bastard might have been hard up drawing in a thrall, but he wasn't completely stupid. The second you and Amy left the alley, he leapt up and took to the roofs. I couldn't keep up with him in my human form."

I bit my bottom lip. "That's why you were so angry when I killed him. Tobias, I'm so sorry. If I had known…"

"If I had wanted you to know, you would have known," he said, stepping in when my words failed me. "I didn't trust you."

"You still don't."

He didn't bother denying it or trying to patronize me. "Why would I? Then again, you haven't reported me to the local matron. I'd know if you had; this area would be crawling with Yellow hoods, trying to figure out who I was and why I was here."

I leaned over the table. "They still might. So, you have any more leads? Crossed any other vamps? Picked up on any other scents?"

"Nothing, but I know she's still here. I get echoes of her every so often. The second I get close to pinpointing her location, though, the feeling disappears. The city… there's too much to hear, too much to smell. My senses are thrown off. As I imagine yours must be."

Truth be told, I could sympathize. I'd passed through large cities before, but never for more than a few hours. My first night in Chicago was a sleepless one. The sounds through the window overwhelmed me. Every hour, a siren, a fight, a cat screeching in the street.

"It took some getting used to, that's for sure. Look, Tobias, I can't make any promises, and I don't know if it will help, but… I know a few vampires on campus."

Fervent eyes across the table glistened. "Where? Who? I have to talk with them."

"Whoa there, Tex."

He'd already gotten halfway out of the booth when I managed to grab his soiled sleeve and drag him back.

"I'm not exactly sure you in your growing lunatic state should be meeting with anyone right now. You go a little too loco and openly attack an innocent vamp, you'll be dead by dawn."

The werewolf across the way chewed on that insult. "But we're stronger than vamps."

"A *pack* is stronger; an individual is going to get his hide sent home in a doggy bag. Just hear me out, okay? You and me, we got a shared interest in this. You're looking for a crèche in the WCU area, and so am I. Whoever sent Donovan after me is still out there. I want questions answered too. Namely, why in the hell do they want me dead?"

"Why haven't you just asked your vampires that question?"

"It's not exactly the kind of thing you bring up right after you start a job. 'Hey, boss, just wondering. I was almost killed twice a few weeks ago by a baby vamp, said his maker ordered him to do it. It's cool, I ripped his head off and stuff, then pretended to be riding his corpse to drive away some homeless guy—'"

Tobias's face screwed up. "You what?"

I waved away the concern. "You had to be there. Anyways, I believe in the saying *don't shit where you live.* But I'm sure I can find an excuse to bring it up on your behalf. Better, even, because then they don't know that *I'm* looking for it too."

White teeth gleamed. Tobias's smile was a thing of beauty. "In a million years, I never thought I'd see the day when a hood helped a wolf. Thank you."

He reached across the table and grabbed both my hands. The moment his flesh touched mine, I felt it again: the bizarre dual sensations of both fire and ice running through my veins. The fire made sense; even I couldn't deny anymore that, at a purely physical level, I found Tobias attractive. If he hadn't been a wolf and I hadn't been a hood, I'd be all over him like sweet on honey. The freezing sensation, however, threw me.

"Where are they? The vampires you know? Can you talk to them tonight?"

I negotiated with the little voice in the back of my head reminding me that the NDA barred me from speaking about the project outside the lab, and that, despite his cheery demeanor, Karmarov could rip my head off like a child decapitating a dandelion if I went about things in an unprofessional manner.

"I'm not working tonight, but I can ask tomorrow."

He scratched the stubble on his chin. "What does that have to do with anything?"

"One of the vamps? He's kind of my boss. I work in Prof. Karmarov's lab, over in the Chem building."

The werewolf, who moments ago had looked at me with a softness usually reserved for Lifetime holiday movies, went cold as Hades. "Really, a lab?"

In a flash, I saw where that instigation was leading. "I'm a hood, Tobias. If there was a werewolf within a block of his lab, I could sense it. I promise you, I haven't picked up the slightest vibration."

"Kara's not part of your local pack. Maybe your senses are off."

"Unlikely, I sense you just fine."

A large hand slicked through his oily black hair. "Maybe if I could sneak in…"

"No. The place has three layers of security, and cameras everywhere. Besides, why would a vampire be holding a werewolf in the Chemistry building? I'm fairly sure the beta is howling at night. Students would hear that."

Tobias huffed, rolling his eyes. "I'm not a freaking bloodsucker, Gerwalta, I don't know why they do the things they do. What is it you work on there?"

"I can't tell you. I signed an NDA."

My words acted as a catalyst, a base being thrown into a vat of highly reactive acid. His grip went from gently coaxing to vicelike. "NDA? What the bloody hell does that mean?"

I explained further. "I started working in Karmarov's lab a week ago. He made me sign a non-disclosure agreement, saying that I wouldn't speak about the project at all."

"Wouldn't… Wouldn't speak about the…"

The crescendo of his tone drew gazes. Hesitant, worried, reluctant men and women who both wanted to intervene, because they thought we were a couple having a fight turned violent, and keep their distance, understanding at some level the predator that Tobias represented.

"This is the closest thing that I've had to a lead since you played pop-goes-the-weasel with Donovan, and you're going to cut me off because you signed a contract?" he huffed. "Look at me. Look at how hard it's getting for me to control myself. She's been away from her pack just as long as I have, and who knows under what kind of conditions. Time is running out for both of us."

"Tobias, you don't even know if the beta is alive."

I'd never seen a man more reverently speak with utter confidence. "She is. I can assure you, she is."

"But if you stay here much longer, you won't be. Look," I whispered as loudly as I dared. "I'll ask the vamps I know, but as a courtesy. I doubt they know anything about a British beta shewolf being kidnapped. And for the love of Van Helsing, *keep your voice down!* People are starting to stare."

Practically throwing my hands back at me, Tobias lounged back in the diner stall, as though reexamining me from a new angle and at a greater distance.

"I was wrong about you," he said at last. "You're not any different at all from the other hoods. In fact, you're worse, because you think you're different. You have all of their weaknesses and none of their strengths."

"If I need to be reminded of my shortcomings, I'll go home and let my mother rip into me. Toblas, honestly, I'm sorry about your brother, and I'm sorry that the other beta is missing. But—"

Leaning in, I called on my nascent power, hoping he could see under the florescent light of the diner the dim blue glow of my eyes. Not that I could muster a real threat if he called me on it, but anything I could do to encourage him to leave wouldn't be in vain.

"You're barking up the wrong tree, if there even is a tree. Come next full moon, if you're still around and can't cross back to your human form, a missing wolf will be the least of your problems. You'll have the Yellow Matron giving her bloodline the order to hunt you down."

"The only hood who knows I'm here is you." With all the coolness of a poker player, he matched my position. Hovering over the table, his eye shone yellow. "I don't think you're eager to be tied up in hood business, which means you'd have to come after me yourself. Make no mistake, if you try to get between me and my mission, I'll huff, and I'll puff, and I'll kill you dead."

Something in his eyes struck fear in me in a way his proximity did not. There was something much more than anger or bravado. There was… sadness. Longing. Desperation. Every moment of his day must be measured in the ticking of the clock. He knew he could save himself. And for some reason, he knew he'd never forgive himself if he left the lost beta behind.

Despite my training and my instincts telling me to match his glare tit for tat, I found myself softening. It must have been evident in my own expression; a moment later, he pulled back and looked at me with a cocked head and a raised eyebrow.

I reached again across the table. "Tobias, she's not in the lab."

My confidence and the table shook when he slammed his palm down on it, cracking the Formica top. "Just mind your own!"

And with that, he rose and chuffed his way out onto the street.

EIGHTEEN

The weight of each sunrise and sunset pulled at my soul. Three days after the encounter in the diner, and I still couldn't shake the memory of Tobias's glare. His words had made a direct demarcation in my life. His eyes haunted me, eyes that begged for something, anything, to give him solace. No matter what I thought, I knew it wasn't in fact a cry for help. Nevertheless, I found myself questioning my place, wondering if it wasn't my duty to aid him, even if he didn't want it.

What would my mother do in this situation? She'd have listened to Tobias fully, then she'd take every clue he could offer, find the missing beta, and destroy them both for good measure. Thank goodness Chicago wasn't my mother's territory. The Head of the House of Yellow, Matron Consuela Renanta, ruled her sanjak with a silver fist and a jaded eye. Nevertheless, she had always been more tempered in her approach to policing the wolves under her jurisdiction than any red hood I knew.

Maybe I should go to her and relay what Tobias had said? If there were two wolves stuck in Chicago against their will and on the edge of moon madness, wouldn't she be the most likely to expediently solve the situation?

No, it wouldn't work, *couldn't* work. As certain as Tobias seemed that Prof. Karmarov was somehow involved or must know something, there was no way he'd agree not to bring up the suspicions if Consuela became involved. There would be no good outcomes if hoods became aware of the genetic profiling and engineering Karmarov was undertaking, even if it had nothing to do with us. Not to mention, it would cost me my job.

What to do? I needed advice, advice from someone who I could trust to keep my worries to himself, who would ask the right questions but not too many questions.

I didn't remember making the decision to dial the phone number when I already found myself listening to the ringing on the other end of the line. When the call connected and I heard my father's voice, however, all my words left me.

"Geri?"

It had been weeks since we'd spoken, and like most conversations since I'd left home, it had been more a brawl than a friendly chat. The sharpness of his absence in my life intensified in the simple fact that he said my name with love every time I called. Each conversation with my dad was a fresh canvas, and he left it up to me what colors and shapes to paint.

"Hi, Papi. I, *um…* I need your help."

"Are you in trouble?"

"No, I'm fine." Taking a deep breath, I gathered myself from the edge of tears. "I need some advice is all."

A smile blossomed in his voice. "Is it about a boy?"

"Kinda." Better he think I had some sort of college crush than learn that I might have to kill a rogue wolf who'd gone over to lunacity. Or worse, help one I barely even knew. "But you have to promise, this stays between us, okay? I don't want Mom knowing anything about it. Especially given what she did."

"You know she was only trying to…"

"I don't care why she did it," I snapped, feeling the bile rise within me. "It was wrong."

"I am not defending your mother's actions." My father's voice softened. His Argentinean accent, usually a thick smoke that blanketed every English word he spoke, weakened. "For what it's worth, Cody is happy. Very happy."

As if that should salve the pain I still felt over losing him. Over being lost to him. Instead of lingering in the heartache, however, I pressed on.

"So, the guy," I said, in as light a tone as I could manage. "He's putting himself out on a limb to help someone, even though it's going to hurt him more to do so than to just walk away."

"A martyr complex," my father declared. "Not unlike your mother."

"My mother?" I asked in disbelief. "Mom is the most selfish woman in the world. You're married to her, you should know."

My father clicked his tongue. "Your mother is many things, but selfish has never been one. Unless you want to talk about taking on the burdens of others, and then she is a glutton."

"I think we'll just need to agree to disagree on that."

Silence came from the other end of the line, until at last he sighed. "In regards to your… *friend.* Sometimes we convince ourselves we alone can make something right. Then, it becomes more than a desire. It becomes a calling, a mission. We think suffering is part of the solution. Sometimes it is, but usually, it's better to share your burdens. We are made stronger by calling on our friendships, never weaker by denying them. The only way to help a martyr is to recognize his struggle, and to help ease it if you can. Just make sure you're not a victim in the process. Now, if you don't mind me asking, as a concerned father of course, is this friend a *boy*friend?"

"No, nothing like that. He's a …"

Werewolf, my mind shouted to complete. I refrained. No need to give my father the impression that history was repeating itself, and certainly no reason to betray Tobias's privacy. My father might be the more compassionate and approachable of my parents, but he was still a hood. Not to mention, he was of the Yellow bloodline. Consuela might be a distant relative, but they still had a connection.

Tobias didn't have to help me out that night in the alley. He didn't have to help me again when Donovan cornered me with orders to kill. He didn't need to let me go the night he'd gotten the better of me in LaBagh Woods. He hadn't had to do a single kind, frankly life-saving, thing that he'd done for me. If for no other reason, I owed him for that.

"I think I know what I need to do then. Thanks, Papi."

"You're welcome, *bonita*. And since you called, I will take advantage of the chance to speak with you and beg you again, come home."

"I can't. Not yet. Maybe not ever."

Something my dad said, however, made me realize I'd be stupid to pass up an opportunity to ask the Red Matron's second a question.

"Hey, Papi, before I came here, I checked the records to see if there was any wolf activity in the city of Chicago itself. There wasn't back then, but it's been a while. By any chance have you…"

"Twice a day," he said before I could get my full question out. "I know you are a big girl, but I am still your father. Of course I look."

The heretofore unnoticed tightness in my chest melted away. "And?"

"No wolves," he said plainly. "Not that I am too concerned. Wolves don't like big, noisy, dirty cities, and Chicago is certainly one of those." Then, pausing, almost as if my silence on the subject suggested something, he added, "Why do you ask?"

"It's nothing," I said, even though it clearly was. Tobias hadn't been lying; no one knew he was here. He either truly was a rogue, or someone had gone through a hell of a lot of work to keep him off the radar. "Just thought I might have sensed… something the other day. But maybe I'm just getting a cold. You know how sometimes I confused the sniffles with the other thing."

My father went to no trouble to cover the suspicion in his tone. "You know, Gerwalta, if you were to come home, go through your rites, your senses would increase and you wouldn't…"

"No," I interjected. "I can't support… Dad, you know what she's doing is wrong."

"My Hilly has her reasons."

Not wanting to insult my father, and all too ready to blast my mother, I decided that was enough. "I have to go, Dad. I have to get to work. Thanks for the advice."

"Of course, *bonita*. Call me back later and tell me if you listened. *Te quiero*."

NINETEEN

"Cynthia?"

The vamp in question only deigned to speak to me when necessary. I'd decided against asking Karmarov about Chicago clutches after his reaction to my initial inquiry regarding crèches. The senior vampire told me the location of his kind's "nurseries" was privileged information, and that as a vamp without a local clutch affiliation, he wasn't in a need-to-know position. Cynthia, however, had reportedly lived in Chicago on and off for the last few decades. She wouldn't give me addresses and local bar reviews, but she might offer up some general information.

"What, hood?"

"I was wondering – just curious, you know, because we don't have such a thing where I come from – are there any crèches around here?"

The olive-skinned researcher held up a slide at eye level, as though not trusting the readout her screen gave her. "There's usually a few in a city big as this. Why? Want to bat for the other team?"

My nose crinkled. "I don't think hoods can be changed."

"Want to feel what it's like to be bitten then? I hear some Hueys find it very pleasurable."

The phantom pain of Donovan's fangs buried in my neck and the pull of his mouth on my blood echoed through my body. My hand went to my neck, rubbing the spot. "Not really. But I wouldn't mind seeing one. You know, just for research. We don't get exposed to much vamp culture way out in the woods."

She turned to me, clearly doubting my thin veil of an excuse. "You know they wouldn't exactly welcome you there, right? A crèche is very tightly protected by its maker. The second they discover what you are, you might not walk away from it – whether or not you mean any harm."

"Would there be a way for you to know what I am unless I told you?" I asked. "Can a vampire sense I'm a hood the way a wolf does?"

"Why would we need to sense hoods?" she said. "You're no threat to us."

Spoken like a person who had never met my mother.

I bit down the impulse to defend my kind. As my father often reminded me in lessons on negotiation, sometimes it was better to be underestimated. Instead, I shrugged and acted as though her insult was water and I was the backside of a duck.

Jess, overhearing the conversation from where he typed research notes on a lab computer, raised an eyebrow. "What about me?" he asked. "Can you sense me?"

What an odd question, I thought. Didn't he know that to Cynthia, he was food? It was like asking a stoner if he could tell when someone was smoking pot nearby.

The vampire's little button nose twitched as she folded her arms and stepped closer to where Jess and I shared a station. Far too bunnylike for a vampire, I thought. Vague memories of reading *Bunnicula* as a child while hiding in the linen closet filled my mind's eye.

After a moment, she crossed her arms over her chest, and surveyed him from the ground up with a scowl. "Yes, but all I get from you when I focus is that you have no fashion sense, and that you probably taste like chicken."

His head tilted down as he tried to pin down what was so off. I agreed with Jess's apparent confusion; in his white Ralph Lauren sweater that let the casual observer pick up on the outline of his chest and a pair of green slacks, I thought he pulled off preppy collegiate pretty damned nice.

And he tasted so much better than chicken.

"Wolves hunt using smell." The vampire grinned, leaning in and running a finger down Jess's chest. "But vampires? We're visual creatures. You'd be better if you left a button or two open on your shirt. Better yet, white tees and tight jeans. No collars."

In a flash, her fangs dropped. Cynthia let out a hiss as she showed off her ready weapons, sending all the blood in Jess's body south and all mine to my head. Was she actually taking him under her thrall right before my eyes? Clearly, this was not a case where being underestimated was going to help me keep what was mine.

I had my blade out of my hair and pressed to the base of her neck before I could manage to blink.

"Try to enthrall my boyfriend, and you and I are going to have a problem, Cindy-Loo Wu."

Clearly an empty threat. I was no match for a vampire in a one-on-one and we both knew it. Fangs aside, if she wanted to go one-on-one in a bitch-off, I was pretty certain I could hold my own.

"Your boyfriend?" Cynthia looked as though she was struggling to swallow laughter, which just made me all the more pissed. With a hiss, her fangs snapped back up into her jaw and she took her hand back. Jess, confused but still lingering in the endorphins enthralling triggered, shook off his confusion. "Well, isn't that sweet?"

The moment Cynthia wandered off, I felt a different type of burning in my cheeks, this time from embarrassment. That turned to anticipation, however, the moment I felt Jess pull me back against him and whisper into my ear.

"So I'm your boyfriend, am I?"

I reached behind me and ran a finger over his cheek. "I was rounding up."

"Do it more. It's very sexy."

Heat blazed through my body. Despite the fact that three vampires were within earshot, I found my back arching as my breath hitched. I turned my head back over my shoulder, licking my lips and all but begging aloud for Jess to kiss me. The pressure of his hands on my hips ticked up as his pupils dilated.

Only a very loud, very insistent, very professorial clearing of a throat across the lab kept me from turning and throwing myself into his arms.

"Miss Kline." Prof. Karmarov didn't look up from the rack of test tubes he was squirting liquids into. "That's not the kind of chemistry we study here."

Both my and Jess's faces crackled into smiles born of frustration and temptation, sealing us together.

"Sorry, professor," I called as we both repositioned ourselves at our station, grabbing two slides each to feed into the machine for scanning.

His eyes focused on his work, Jess whispered, "Later, maybe."

I knew he was keeping his voice down because he assumed the vamps wouldn't be able to hear it. I, however, knew better. "They can hear everything we're saying."

I looked over to the table where Kai and Cynthia worked at inhuman speeds, marking up slides on their display. Cynthia remained as mushmouthed as ever, but the corner of Kai's mouth ticked up, providing evidence for my presumption.

"I don't care," Jess said. "It's none of their business."

A whole tropical rain forest full of butterflies fluttered in my stomach. "I know, but it's a bad call to try and get to third base with your boyfriend at work, even if you can blame it partially on the fault of it being that time of month."

Jess's face screwed up, and I rewound the record in my head to figure out why.

"I mean the moon phases," I quickly amended. "The hormones go completely out of whack, and the closer to a full moon, the wilder I get."

I blushed over when I saw the mix of wonder and, if I wasn't mistaken, strategizing in his eyes.

"Don't think you're going to take advantage of that, Jess Harmond," I warned, though the smile in my voice matched the one on my face. "I still can't believe I'm telling you stuff like this."

"Some sort of family secret?" he asked.

I swallowed a laugh. "Hardly. We're not exactly chatty about stuff in my family. The only time I brought it up with my mom she completely shut down. It was like I was asking her which sexual position was the best one."

Jess grinned. "I'd be happy to discuss that one with you too."

TWENTY

Dear Miss Kline,

Reports are that your work on the Helsing Helix program has been exemplary, and it is therefore with great honor that I confirm your internship with White-Whitman Labs this summer. Your appointment will commence one week following the end of the spring academic term, and will conclude one week prior to the beginning of the fall term. In addition, you will have up to five days of your choosing as personal enrichment and/ or vacation days through the summer. You will be responsible for setting your own schedule, but you must dedicate at least thirty hours per week in the lab, of which at least one shift must fall between 10 PM and 4 AM. You will be compensated at your current stipend rate, plus 25%. You will also be eligible for a summer-end bonus for completing your internship.

Congratulations on all your hard work, and welcome to the project.

Inga Rosethorn, Internship Coordinator, White-Whitman Labs.

"Inga Rosethorn?"

I read the name out loud, enunciating like a student in a language lab training his mouth on new vocabulary. It wasn't that I didn't know the name. It was that I knew it too well.

"Not *the* Inga Rosethorn?"

Across the desk from me, Prof. Karmarov twirled in his old-school, wooden office chair, a risqué piece of furniture given that the material was one of the few that could penetrate vampire flesh and kill them.

"I suppose my answer to that depends on your clarification."

Was he being deliberately difficult, or just setting me up to give away what I knew?

"The most powerful vampire in Central Europe?"

The corner of his mouth ticked in annoyance. "Well, then, the answer to that is no. She doesn't live in Central Europe anymore. She relocated to Chicago two years ago."

"Holy shit, Vlad's firstborn?"

My voice bounced off of brick walls. Slapping my hands over my mouth, Karmarov shooed away my immediate concern.

"Cynthia and Kai are on an errand. I doubt very much that Jess heard you." He leaned over his desk nonetheless, as if there was still a reason to be discreet despite what he'd just said. "I'm not sure how *you* know that, but most vampires don't. It would be wise to keep that knowledge to yourself."

"I'm sorry, I didn't know. I…" I took a pickaxe to my memory, trying to dig out the context. "I think I was at her house once, as a child when I was visiting Germany with my mother."

One of Karmarov's eyebrows arched. "*You* met Inga Rosethorn?"

Funny, he'd only said *you* yet I heard so much more than that.

"Being the Red Matron's daughter has privileges. And I don't know if I actually met her. I just remember having to get very dressed up and thinking the food at her house sucked." But he was missing my obvious question. "What in the world is someone like Inga Rosethorn doing working as the internship coordinator at a Chicago biomed lab?"

"You probably think someone of her stature would have a very high-profile title, don't you?" Karmarov asked. "CEO or Director, perhaps?"

"I've always been led to believe that vamps are really into prestige." Insofar as my education had covered topics to do with the undead, a primary theme had been the importance they placed on deference and the perception of —if not actual— dominance.

"Amongst our own, perhaps. But in a position requiring interaction with the Huey world, it's sometimes best for our more prominent luminaries to hide in plain sight. Meanwhile, behind the scenes, they're the ones running the show."

In the back of my mind I thought about a brilliant genetics researcher who could have easily gotten tenure at any Ivy League institute instead of settling into the unassuming role of an assistant professor at a fairly insignificant regional university.

Was Prof. Karmarov hiding in plain sight? If so, hiding from what?

Whatever. As far as I could tell, Karmarov spent all his waking hours not teaching his one course in the evenings, in the lab. Did he ever actually leave this building? The work he was heading to tap out slayer DNA was already a hidden motive; I couldn't possibly imagine he had time to have a triple life going on.

"Cool. Hoods mostly just take jobs where they interact with the packs in day-to-day settings. You know, like bankers or teachers or veterinarians."

"Veter…" The word died and his lips curled into a smile when he realized the joke. "Ha! Because they're…. Right, well, yes. I suppose that makes sense. Wolves and hoods tend to settle in rural areas or small towns; vamps and slayers in large cities. Well, slayers did until…" He sighed. "But that doesn't matter now. I'm close, Miss Kline. I can feel it. Soon, we'll have enough complete sequences that we can move to phase two."

"Phase two?" I scooted to the front of my chair. "What's phase two?"

"Developing gene therapies, of course. Ones that could perhaps trigger the slayer abilities in adults with an existing genetic predisposition."

"I'm sorry, professor, a *predisposition*?"

He shied. "I imagine despite all your kind's attempts to keep procreation within your community, there's been a hood or two who's gone looking beyond the edge of the firelight and ended up with something to show for it."

"One famous one in particular."

Any humor in his eyes died. "My apologies, I didn't mean to imply something like *Die Verräterin*. What I mean is, there are humans with a slayer somewhere in their family tree. Our goal would be to identify those individuals and recruit them, if appropriate, into a genetic therapy trial. We're also looking at the possibility of a genetically engineered infant. We could literally birth a new generation of slayers. Genetics is amazing. So many possibilities, so many ways to correct our wrongs."

"You know, Test Tube Slayers wouldn't be a bad band name."

This time, the smile failed to break across his face. I took that as my cue to leave.

"Anyway," I sighed, holding up the letter. "I suppose I should get downstairs and get back to work if I want to hit the ground running this summer. Thanks, Professor. Please tell White-Whitman that I'm delighted to accept their offer."

An hour later, as I stood side by side with Jess in the lab, I could still feel the effervescence tingling my inside. The letter stuffed in my nearby backpack filled the room with helium and any second, I would break out into an epic giggling fit. A job. *I* had an actual job in Chicago.

Until now, I'd been afraid that I was going to have to take up Rick Ryland's offer to work at the state park for the summer, as I had previously. That would mean going back to Paradise, a town much too small to hide from two people I vehemently did *not* want to see: my mother, and my ex-boyfriend, Cody.

"What has you so giddy?" Jess asked without looking away from the slide he was pulling from the scanning machine.

A hammer shattered my bubble. What if Jess hadn't also been offered work for the summer? What if there had only been one position, and I had gotten it? What if he hated me when he found out? It was funny: even though Jess and I had only known each other for less than two months, and even though we'd only gotten to the point of calling each other a couple in the last few days, he'd already fashioned himself a little comfortable nook in my isolated life. Suddenly, the idea that he'd not be there had me panicked. My chest felt tight as I attempted to iron out any abrupt signs of emotion from my voice.

"Jess, what are you doing this summer?"

He shrugged. "Haven't thought much about it. Dr. K was talking to me the other day about maybe staying on with the project over the summer. Why?"

The ache under my ribs melted in a warm gush. "Thank god."

Something in my voice must have tipped him off. The slide pinched in his fingers tinkled as he dropped it back into the tray. He turned and reached for me, as if by instinct, knowing I needed comfort.

"Come on, now." With a gentle pull, he wrapped me in his arms. "What's all this for?"

"Nothing, just…"

His finger pressed to my lips. "You were scared I was going to take off for the summer and find myself someone else? Someone better than a badass hood, like maybe a yeti or something?"

My anxiety immediately turned to frustration. I play-slapped his chest. "There's no such thing as yetis!"

"You're not supposed to exist either, but you feel real to me."

The proximity of him, the yearning that burned inside me that I hadn't felt in ages, that I swore I could never feel again, roared to life. Not content to let his kiss be a mere touch of lips, I laced my hand through his hair and kept his mouth working against mine, massaging his kiss and coaxing the flames of desire within him. Within *us.*

I only stopped when my more sensitive ears picked up on what I was sure was a very intentional book drop in the office upstairs.

"It's impossible to get away with anything naughty when vampires are nearby," I said, smiling against him.

"I know," Jess replied.

"Good thing there's only another hour to our shift. Maybe we can go somewhere where *no one* will hear us."

"Just so you know—" Karmarov's voice found its way down the winding staircase. "I'm going to close this door for a while so I can concentrate. Please try to control yourselves. I understand you're both college students, but seriously…"

Looking at each other, we both struggled not to laugh from the awkwardness. Jess unwove his arms and turned back to the table, closing the lid of the box he'd been working on while I was meeting upstairs with Prof. Karmarov.

"Or we might be done now. We finished scanning and cataloging all the slides on this tray. We need another, but Kai and Cynthia are gone. No way to get into the refrigeration room."

"Karmarov can probably let us in." Glancing over at the vampires' workstation, however, I caught a glint of light that reflected off a set of keys.

I crossed the lab to the vamps' workstation and grabbed Cynthia's set of keys. "She left these behind. Are these only lab keys? I thought they had her house key on them too."

Jess didn't seem as concerned as me. He shrugged. "Maybe she left them on purpose so we could get another tray. She's constantly on our backs for being so slow, but even she had to realize we'd get through the first one by ourselves with time to spare – even without superhuman speed."

"Speak for yourself, slowpoke. I *am* superhuman." Barely. Not as much as I'd be if I finally ceded to my parents' wishes – my mother's *demands* – and completed the hooding rites.

With one balled fist planted on a hip and the others jingling the keys, I contemplated the options. One, head back upstairs and beg Karmarov for permission. Doable, but wouldn't we come off as little kids who felt like they needed to ask permission to turn on the TV? After basically just being told to mind our raging hormones and not touch each other in inappropriate places, not really a dynamic I wanted to reinforce. Or, I could just grab out another of the trays from the shelf and Jess and I could actually get our work done. And maybe, just maybe, Jess wouldn't refuse if I suggested he walk me home, or laugh at me if I invited him to come upstairs for a few minutes.

After all, Amy would be gone tonight. She'd moved on – and, more or less over the last few weeks, moved in – with her latest featured boyfriend flavor. Not that I expected that to last. Still, Jess and I could take advantage of the situation to Netflix and Chill.

Hell, we'd been getting so hot lately, chilling was the only thing we had left to do.

I caught a mischievous grin on Jess's face and knew he was thinking the same thing. With one toss and catch of the keys, I crossed the room to a metal door with a head-sized viewing window and covered over in a new layer of brown paint with every change in the White House since Eisenhower. I'd never been in here – both Cynthia and Kai had insisted on refreshing our supplies whenever we ran low. As expected, wire shelving units held several dozen encyclopedia-sized trays. I entered and went right when suddenly, my insides rebelled. I felt like a fist had grabbed onto my belly button and twisted.

"Whoa!"

My hand caught the shelf next to me just in time to keep me from falling. My other hand laced over my stomach, as though trying to keep the contents in place.

What the hell was this? Did the vampires booby trap the fridge somehow? I knew Prof. Karmarov's work required a certain level of security, but if it was really this important, they wouldn't possibly have left the keys to the assets just sitting around like that, would they?

My lingering inside the fridge must have worried Jess. The next moment, as I struggled to stay on my feet, I heard him call out.

"Everything okay, Geri?"

What was I going to say? *No, I think there's some kind of chemical defense in here; hurry up so it can get you too?*

As a hood, I wasn't immortal in the way vamps were, and I didn't have the physical resilience of a wolf, especially as a nascent, but my biological fortitude was more robust than any Huey's. If whatever in this fridge was having this effect on me, it'd probably knock Jess right on his ass.

I focused on the box of slides nearest the entry despite its composition where the others were plastic, gave myself a 1.8-second internal pep talk, grabbed it, and bolted.

And plowed smack dab into Jess's chest.

His hands braced my shoulder, keeping both me and the box containing the tray from crashing to the ground.

"What happened? You look as white as a ghost."

A corner of my mouth twitched. "Oh, the charm..."

A moment later, the weight lifted from my hands as Jess took the box under one arm, and looped the other around my waist, guiding me out. He groaned as he tried to close the door behind him with a foot.

"Jesus Christ, that thing is heavy. What's it made of, lead?"

The box with the tray tinkled as he set it on the table, making me fill with dread. Had the slides inside come out of their slots? Had they broken? Remembering how Karmarov said they had been collected – mostly postmortem – at great expense from around the world, I felt the roil in my stomach intensify.

"Jess, the slides…"

"Can wait," he interjected, now turning his attention to me. His strong hands braced my shoulders as he pushed me down on a lab stool. Three iterations of his face swam in my vision as I tried to focus on the middle one. "What happened?"

My voice sounded raspy, winded, as though I'd just finished running ten miles. "There's some sort of booby trap, a chemical barrier or something, in that room. The vamps wouldn't be affected by it. I should've… I should've guessed they'd do something like that."

Jess's back straightened. He looked to the fridge's entry across the room, narrowing his eyes. "Why would they need to booby trap the fridge? You sure you just didn't knock something over?"

"No, I would have heard if I did, even if it was small. Oh, my god. Jess, you came to the door, you breathed the air. Are you okay?"

His face scrunched up, as though he'd just realized that fact the same moment I did. He looked himself over, like signs would be smeared across his shirt. "I feel fine. I was only at the door; you were all the way inside."

True. Still, my resistance to such things should have been five times his.

"Jess, can you open that tray of slides?"

His hands dropped to his sides. "What? Why?"

Gaining my feet on shaky legs, circling behind the stool and using It to prop myself up, I struggled with my equilibrium. Only one thing ever had this kind of effect on me – being close to a werewolf, one that was emotionally distraught.

"Please, Jess, Just open the box."

He took two steps back to the worktable. Keeping his eyes fixed on me, as though expecting my head to explode or something, Jess reached out and slowly, slowly tipped the box open.

A wave crashed over me, a blind force pushing me down. Their pain, their torment, their fear, their hate. It fed into my soul, the gut-wrenching torment of a century of wolves, brought to a bitter end.

I didn't know how I knew, only *that* I knew. These slides were from werewolves who had all lost their mates.

I fled, crossing the room and heading straight to the elevator, pushing the button over and over.

Jess, horror-stricken, slammed the box shut and ran to me. "Holy shit, what the hell? I've never seen anyone move so fast."

"Werewolves!" I said, my voice tight.

He pivoted, doing a full three-sixty. "Where?"

My hand stretched out, one finger targeting the source of my disruption across the room. "Those blood samples. They're not slayers. They're all werewolves. I have to… I need to go home."

Jess became a rock at my side. I leaned in, clutching at the fabric of his shirt. His eyes were full of concern and laced with panic when I looked up at him. "I'm taking you home."

Without another word, my feet swept out beneath me as Jess's arms caught me. I cradled next to his body as he walked us into the elevator.

"Miss Kline, Mr. Harmond – what's going on? I thought I heard a scream. I…"

Prof. Karmarov's puzzled expression, seeing us staring back at him from the elevator as he stood frozen on the stairs, was like looking at a still life. I wondered if, from his perspective, it looked like Jess and I had been caught in another of our borderline amorous moments. Something in the way I was clinging to Jess, like he was rescuing me, must have tipped him off. His gaze pivoted, landing next at the workstation where the slides full of werewolf DNA still sat.

His wide eyes swung an arc from the table back to me. "Gerwalta, I—"

Instinct must have pushed the scream from my throat. I had been trained since a babe in diapers to anticipate a werewolf attack, to mentally steel myself for a lycanthropic onslaught. Vampires, however, were another thing altogether. I had no sufficient defense. If he came for me, I would die.

Jess's arms tightened around me. We swung, Jess pivoting on the spot so that his body protected me. Never mind that I was the stronger of the two of us, that I would be the one who could at least stand up to a vampire, even if I knew I wouldn't be able to persevere in such a battle. Jess, however? He'd be nothing more than flesh food.

And yet, he protected me. He placed himself between me and danger.

I'd never felt more afraid and more overwhelmed by appreciation in my life than at the moment I realized I was falling for Jess, and that Prof. Karmarov's fangs were bare as he leapt in our direction, an arm outstretched to grab me the second he got close enough.

The elevator doors closed just as a tremendous thud slammed into the outer metal doors.

TWENTY-ONE

The ceramic mug warmed my hands, casting out chills that racked my body after the initial adrenaline had burned away.

Jess laid his hand on my knee as we sat on the couch. "You couldn't have known."

"I could have." I buried my chin in my chest. I didn't want him looking in my eyes. He'd see my shame, and as fragile as I felt at the moment, I didn't know that I'd be able to keep from telling him the truth. I did know. Tobias told me. Only, I refused to listen.

With two fingers crooked under my chin, Jess lifted my gaze to meet his. "I promise, whatever it is, I won't tell anyone." Then, choking out a laugh, he added, "You think I go around telling people I've spent the last two months working nights in a secret lab in the Browning Building with three vampires and a hood?"

Of course, he didn't.

"What is it about that tray that upset you so much? And don't just say it's because they were werewolf samples. That doesn't come close to telling me what's actually going on."

The lump in my throat doubled in size. With dull eyes, I studied Jess's features, noting both his compassion and concern. A furrowed brow deepened as the clench of his jaw tightened. His hand, still on my knee, massaged gently, kneading a patch of flesh warmed by his efforts. He wanted to help me, to understand. He was being there for me, as cliché as that sounded. And I realized, only by showing him my weakness, could he truly understand my strength.

He was worthy. He had put himself between me and an attacking vampire. He didn't ask why I needed to leave or try to argue me out of it; he just helped me do what I needed to do.

Closing my eyes, I sucked in a deep breath through my nose before pushing it, and the truth, out in a fine stream. "I'm not like other hoods."

A glimmer of a smile twitched on his lips. "Since you're the only one I've ever met, I'm going to need you to expand on that."

"All hoods have certain skills," I continued. "Innate strengths. But after our rites, after the Gate of Fire, they're off the charts on the human scale."

"Sounds more exciting than catechism," he joked.

"A few of us can even…" I swallowed down my nerves, hoping this wasn't the stone that was going to crumble any credulity he allowed me. "…fly."

"Fly?" Jess's eyes went from thin slits to white orbs floating in a red cloud. "What, like Superman, or something?"

"Why do you think superheroes have capes?" I teased. "It's taken from us. Or, at least, we think it is. You see, we're called hoods because we actually do wear hooded capes. The weird thing is though, they're kind of… um, magic."

How much more of this could I tell him without him running, screaming through the door, never to talk to me again?

"You've heard how werewolves can be killed with silver, right?"

"Isn't that the popular story? A silver bullet to the heart?"

I nodded. "But did you ever wonder how that was done before guns were invented?"

Jess shrugged. "I assumed with spears, or really, really good slingshots."

"I *am* thoroughly trained in archery. In fact, the wrist bow is my favorite weapon. Hard to wear it around Chicago without getting looks, though. But a hood doesn't need anything but the silver. We can wield silver."

Jess's forehead wrinkled. "What does that mean, *wield* silver? Like you hold it out in front of you or something? Hate to break it to you, but Hueys are pretty good at that too."

"I'm sure you're very good at holding silver, dear, but what I mean is, we can manipulate it, command it. After we go through the Gate of Fire, silver obeys us. We can shape it into anything we want. We don't need a gun to shoot a wolf in the heart. We just need a bit of silver and proximity. FYI, either the brain or the heart is fatal. The brain is usually easier to reach."

He held up his hands, enumerating the facts so far on his fingers. "So hoods can kick ass; wield silver; hear, smell, and move faster than humans – excuse me, *Hueys;* a few can fly, and… anything else?"

"That's pretty much it. Except…" I sighed, running my hands through my hair. "Like I said, I'm special. I have a particular skill my mother wanted to utilize. I can sense wolves."

Whatever anticipation had been building in his eyes deflated like a balloon zipping across the room. "Sense wolves? Is that all?"

Was he serious? "Think how useful that would be to a woman whose job includes hunting down troubled wolves to kill. All hoods can sense when one is within a dozen feet or so, but that's not much better than using your eyes, is it? But me? Sometimes a half-mile away. Not as much here in the city, though. I don't know if it's all the buildings or because there are so many people, but I only get a few blocks here. My mother believes, if I went through rites, I could have a sense of proximity unlike any hood that's ever come before."

Proving that Jess loved playing Devil's advocate, he kept drilling for the importance of this seemingly insignificant ability. "Does she have a constant need to track down and kill wolves? From what you said before, the role of a hood is more of a deterrent."

"It *should* be."

It used to be.

Setting the half-empty cup of cooling tea on the side table, I tucked my feet up underneath me and turned toward Jess.

"But the supe world has gone high tech. My mother and her cabal believe the best deterrent is total control. Shortly after I was born, they started a registry. They pitched it to the packs as a way to expand their communities without all the risks and costs involved in travel. A way to find new mates and keep their traditions alive. They registered in droves. But what it's turned into is a way for self-righteous hoods to control pack movements. It's as good as 'Show me your papers' in the dark days of Europe."

Understanding dawned in Jess's features. He may have been a chem student, but he had a basic understanding of social science. "And let me guess, the packs have retaliated by hiding from the registry, by not reporting themselves. And your ability to perceive them…"

"Makes it harder for them to hide," I said, completing his thought. "But it gets worse. My mother is the Matron of the Red Hoods. Matrons have unrestricted and *unmonitored* access to our history and archives. She says there's a precedent for someone with my talent. When they took rites, not only did their range and degree of perception increase, but they could throw the sensory direction in reverse. Basically, they could make themselves into a beacon that the wolves could sense."

"To trap them," Jess said. "Like setting out a leg of lamb tainted with poison."

"Exactly. So, I've put off taking rites. I don't want to be that. I don't want to be her tool to clamp down on innocent families. I don't want to be part of their system of control."

My soul sighed when, after a few moments of mental digestion, Jess opened his arms and invited me in. In all the years since my mother had shared her vision for my future – *our* future, she'd put it – I had only opened up to one other person. In that case, only after years of building trust, of knowing he wouldn't use the information against either me or my family, did I accept him as part of my life. When I found out the potential I held, his curious reaction had been to comfort me as well. As I fell into Jess's hold, as his arms circled around me and he gently rocked me from side to side, the recollection of that moment when I finally had a confidant doubled back on me, up to, and including, the moment that it had all been taken away.

Cody. With a she-wolf. Mated.

At my mother's insistence.

Sweet turned sour in my mouth, and my body went rigid.

Jess stopped on a dime, but he didn't pull away. "Did I do something wrong?"

"No!" How could I let this ghost rise up between us? Jess was trying to support me, and all I could do was push my damage between us. "It's not you. It's…"

But my words died, along with any hope that I'd ever get over what my mother had done to me. I didn't remember tearing up, but as I pulled myself out of Jess's arms and wiped a sleeve over my cheek, I pulled it away to find the splotch of dark gray where my tears had wet the fabric.

Jess swept a warm palm over my cheek, cupping my face and drawing my eyes to his. "Whoever it is you're remembering and whatever it was they did to you, I'm not them."

The corners of my mouth twitched. "You're psychic now?"

"I don't need supernatural abilities to see that you're hurting." He pulled my face forward just enough to ghost a kiss over my lips. "What your mother did to you what she expected you to do– is horrible. But I'm sure she only did it because deep down, she thought it was the best way to protect you. With a power like that, and if your kind really has become so restrictive of the wolves, I don't doubt that would make you a target." Another light kiss, and he swept the hair that had fallen in my face away as he beamed at me. "It's a good thing the wolves don't know."

I sucked on my bottom lip before whimpering, "One does."

Compassion turned to a critical need to protect. Jess's jaw went rigid as his hand dropped away. "Who?"

"My ex-boyfriend, Cody."

I didn't know if it was because he could see the lingering emotions in my eyes or if that my ex was a werewolf that made Jess prickle. His muscles tightened under his skin, as he labored to keep his expression neutral.

"We broke up last year," I clarified. "I'm sure if he wanted to use what he knows about me for any nefarious purpose, he would have done so by now."

Confusion still marred his features. "From everything you told me before, I don't understand how that even happens. How does a hood end up in a relationship with a werewolf? Aren't you guys like the Hatfields and McCoys?"

"We don't exactly have family picnics together." I shrugged. "Small town dynamics. Paradise has less than a thousand people in it. Between hoods and werewolves blending into the Huey population, choices are few. Plus, I suppose Cody was sort of my teenage rebellion. We started dating our senior year of high school. I guess at first I was using him to piss off my mom, and he didn't mind – another chance for a werewolf to tick off a hood. But we actually hit it off. We were together almost two years."

"And why did you…" In a guttural click, he cleared his throat. "Why did you two break up?"

I arched an eyebrow. "Is that relevant?"

Defiance defined his stance as he laced his arms over his chest. "Just want to know if there's some asshole out there with an axe to grind, or who might hold some sort of petty jealousy if… when he finds out we're together."

"You don't need to worry," I assured him, putting a hand on his knee. "He's married now."

"That may be true, but…"

My hand went up, stopping his words. "No, you don't get it. Wolves mate for life – that goes for both the purebred animal and for the supernatural hybrid. Once a wolf consummates with a mate, adultery is a biological impossibility. Their DNA won't allow for it."

"Yeah, but you and he…" Jess coughed out, framing what he thought was an obvious end result of a long-term romance. When he caught the hurt look in my eyes, his smile fell. "Really, not even once?"

"The consequences… I always thought it would be so selfish of me. The moment we – *you know* – he would be bound to me for life, but I could change my mind at any time, leaving him trapped. Or if I was killed doing my duties… You've never been around a werewolf who's lost his mate, Jess. You can't understand the pain they go through. Think if I left him on purpose, what that would do to him? Most lone wolves we encounter separate from their packs on purpose. Death by hood is something I've heard of a few times. With me and Cody—I loved him too much to ever put him in that kind of situation. And then, he mated Lisa, and any romantic feelings he had for me… They're all irrelevant now. *I'm* irrelevant now."

"Actually, you're pretty much the only thing I care about right now." In a bold, quick move for a Huey, Jess pulled my hand from his mouth before stroking my cheek. "So, you're a… I mean, are a … What I mean is…"

"Yes, Jess, I'm a virgin."

He went wide-eyed at my bluntness.

"Don't act like it's a big deal, because it isn't." No matter what Amy thought. "I'm not ashamed or proud of it, and it's not something I'm holding on to out of any sort of sentimentality or moral code. The situation has just never happened."

He looked like he was trying to swallow a fishbowl. "I… Gerwalta, I want to…" Finally, he swallowed down his nerves, sat up straight, and turned towards me. "I'm not saying right now or today or even anytime soon, but when you're ready to…"

I didn't even let him finish the sentence. All it took was me remembering how this defenseless Huey, oblivious to how easily a vampire like Karmarov could have eviscerated him, put himself between us without hesitation. I remembered how he'd come into our crazy world, where there were such things as vampires and hoods and werewolves, and hadn't even blinked. The man who could dive into the deep end of the pool and break to the surface of the water without even gasping, who put my safety over his sanity, was a man I wouldn't soon let go.

I crushed my lips to his with a ferocity even I hadn't known was possible. After blinking away his confusion at the sudden move, Jess kissed me back, his hand raising to lace through my hair, angle my head, and deepen our connection. Without breaking away, I drew myself up and threw a leg over his lap. As I straddled him, places I'd let go dormant within me sparked to life, and I felt my senses – all of them – awaken.

"Geri?" He pulled back, looking up at me with awe. "Your eyes are glowing blue."

I nodded. "That happens whenever my primal instincts are aroused."

"Primal instincts?" A seductive grin parted as he ran the tip of his tongue over his top lip. "I like the sound of that."

His hands made their way under my shirt. With lithe fingers, he traced lines over my ribs, circled around my back, and unhooked my bra – all while kissing me with a languid patience that made the ache growing in my belly more pressing. Would he take off my shirt, or did he expect me to do it? He'd have to give up my mouth first, and Jess seemed to have no intention of doing anything like that.

The next moment, however, when his hands came back around and he used the pads of his thumbs to entice my desire, I threw back my head and gasped. Too long. It had been too damn long since I'd felt like this. God, I'd missed it.

With one corner of his mouth arched, he leaned in to kiss my neck. "If my fingers do that to you, imagine what my mouth is going to feel like."

Oh, Valhalla. In my mind's eye, I pictured him carrying out the task. Heat shot down my spine. Suddenly, my moaning altered, becoming a gruff grunt.

Not because I had had any sort of negative reaction, and not because I wasn't close to going over the edge from just a little bit of foreplay, but because I'd suddenly picked up on the presence of a werewolf.

One who, based on how strong I could sense his proximity, was more than likely just on the other side of my front door.

My hands became fists as I shifted my weight and climbed down from Jess's lap, leaving him in a comical pose, kissing air. I'd unsheathed the silver blade hidden in my hair by the time he'd shaken off the confusion and stood.

"What? What is it?"

With a slash across my mouth, I signaled Jess to stay quiet. Not that it would matter. Even if Tobias hadn't heard him, he more than certainly could smell Jess.

Pointing at the door, I mouthed the word "werewolf" and signaled for Jess to stay where he was. Then, I turned around, the knife held out in a striking position.

"What do you want, Tobias?"

For a moment, all I could hear was his breathing in response. Quick, shallow, racing – as though he'd just run a marathon.

"Tobias?" The blade dropped a little lower as concern replaced my annoyance. "Why are you even still here? I thought you left Chicago. Didn't you and I discuss the consequences if you go lunar?"

"I found her."

I didn't need to ask who; that much was obvious.

"Okay, but what do you…"

"I need your help," he said, his breaths evening out. "I can't get to her. I… tried… and I… It's dark, and I think she's…"

Suddenly all my heistance disappeared, replaced by a nagging concern that even I didn't understand. He was losing his humanity already. I'd never seen a wolf go through the process of going moon mad; I'd only seen the final result when, stripped of the ability to hold a primate form, one struggled to connect with his humanity, and even then, only from a distance, safely behind my mother's warrior pose.

"Tobias, you need to go home. Please, don't do this to yourself."

Don't do this to me.

His voice cracking, he sounded as though he were on the edge of tears. "I know where she's being held. I need to save her. I need to save her and… I don't know. She's been away from her pack for too long, but she's a beta. Maybe she's stronger. Maybe she can come out of the wolf for one more cycle. But me… If I don't, there won't be enough of my human mind left to save her. I have to free her. You have to help me."

Was he really rambling on like this, knowing I had a Huey in the room with me? How crushing was his desperation, to chance exposure like that? Knowing it was a bad idea, and knowing I'd regret it in the long run, I reached out, took the door knob in hand, and slowly leveraged it open.

And that was when the world went black.

TWENTY-TWO

"Is she going to be okay?"

"Why do you care?"

"I don't. Just seems like a waste, you know, given what she said about what she can do."

Voices reverberated off walls I could not see, before crashing into a void. One man, one woman, both speaking at ease just beyond where my body had been strewn out over a cold, stone floor. Either they didn't know I was awake, or it didn't matter.

The woman's voice, laced with contempt, continued. "She's too valuable to damage too much. For now, anyway."

The voices grew faint, moving away as my mind labored to focus on their timbre and tones. Both were so familiar, but placing them proved just out of reach; either because the way it reverberated cloaked it from my recollection, or because my brain had been scrambled when someone hit me over the head.

Speaking of which... *fucking ow.*

With a shaky hand, my fingers inspected the crown of my head. Dried blood caked my hair, but the wound had already begun to heal. I must have been hit. Or maybe I fell down and hit my head? Yeah, how likely was that? What happened? One minute I was mauling Jess, thinking I'd finally make Amy proud, and the next...

Jess! Oh, my god, what about Jess? Panic took me to my feet, and across the room. Fist a-flailing, I pounded the thick glass wall, beating out a fervent rhythm and screaming at the top of my lungs.

"What did you do with Jess? He's just a Huey, you bastards!" More fist thumping, more useless braying. "I swear, if you've hurt one single hair on his head."

The two who had been conversing grew suspiciously quiet. Above me, electronic gears clicked. The sound was one with which I was overly familiar. A remote-controlled security camera repositioned to take me in. Behind me, the recognizable old brickwork that made up the exterior of the Browning Building, but filtered through another wall set before it, one that seemed to be both thick and clear, like some sort of glass. It was mirrored in front of me as well. Both walls to the left and right appeared to be made of concrete, and none of them in any direction had a visible door that I could see, leaving me to wonder how I'd come to be deposited here.

"What is this, some kind of racquetball court?"

Instinct told me I wasn't here by chance, and no way was this something Hueys were behind. Supes were involved, no two ways about it. I reached up to my braid, loose but still woven on the back of my head, and felt for the hilt of my constant weapon.

No sheath, no knife. Nothing. Whoever had taken us knew the decorative clip in my hair wasn't merely for fashion's sake; it hid one of my only defenses.

As I turned my head, my braid scraped across my shoulders, teasing the skin just under my cotton shirt. It reminded me of Jess's touch, which in turn reminded me of his voice. And in that moment, I knew who was talking just out of sight.

"Jess?"

He slipped into my field of vision and stood in front of the glass wall. My eyes cataloged him, looking for any signs he'd been injured. My boyfriend was pristine, not a scratch on him. But the way he looked at me, detached from any warmth or familiarity, told me something was off-kilter. Suddenly, the truth hit me.

My hand massaged my wound. "It was you."

"In fairness, I was aiming for the wolf," he acknowledged. "But when you heard my tranq gun fire, you dove in front of him, pushed him out of the way. You hit your head when you fell."

"You were trying to get Tobias?" My words rang in my head.

"I've been after him the whole time. He was my mission. You were bait."

Looking around at my surroundings, other truths fell into place. I was a prisoner, and after a moment, I even realized where. Jess had told me it himself that day we first met, hadn't he? How there were supposedly secret labs under Browning where animals had been experimented on in the war era. I was in a holding pen. Sending out my senses, however, I didn't pick up on any wolf in the area.

Tobias had gotten away.

My gaze held his as I sent all the animosity I'd kept from my voice out through my glare. "I don't believe you. You're not that smart."

He sizzled under my attention, shifting his weight and staring at the floor. A moment later, he was no longer alone. Cynthia appeared with preternatural speed, crossing her arms and cocking a hip.

"No, Little Red, but I am." Cynthia sneered, clicking her tongue. "He was told to distract you from what any decently trained hood would have picked up on in the lab. If he had had half a brain and gone into the fridge himself to get another tray of slides instead of letting you do it, you never would have stumbled onto the werewolf samples. Lucky for him it led to you two being in the right place, at just the right time."

The werewolf genetic samples, I'd almost forgotten about them. My mind indexed everything that had happened leading up to the moment where the sorrow of dozens of wolves pressed on the edges of my consciousness. The box had been so heavy because it had been made of silver.

But how had they come to have werewolf samples? The hoods and the wolves had agreed together, that unlike vampires who could mind trick their way out of explaining their unique physical traits, we would have no such luck. We went to extreme lengths to make sure our genetic information never went outside our communities. Something still didn't add up, and I had a feeling the missing numbers to balance this equation lay in the unknown quantities of Cynthia's cryptic statement.

"Right time and right place for what?" I asked.

She grinned, the way one does at a child who'd figured out how to get on the counter and break into the cookie jar: with equal parts appreciation and malice.

"You were never supposed to be part of this project, Geri," Cynthia said. "I only let you come on board because Karmarov insisted you'd be of value to him. *I* don't care about restoring the slayer lines. I don't care, because…" She reached behind her, stroking a hand under Jess's cheek like she was teasing a dog's muzzle. "Not *all* of them are gone."

No. No way. It couldn't be. I appraised Jess with newfound understanding. "You're a slayer?"

For the first time since revealing himself as an accomplice, he smiled. "My father was one of the last."

So he was half-slayer. I leaned forward. "That puts me in a bit of a quandary, doesn't it? I'm pretty sure it would be a bad thing for me to kill an endangered animal, and yet, I so want you dead."

His cocky grin mocked me. "An hour ago, you were ready to sleep with me."

"Yeah, well, an hour ago I didn't know you were scum, so…"

Cynthia's hand flew up, shooing Jess away. "Run along now, dear. I have some things to ask Little Red here."

I'd find a way for Jess to get his comeuppance eventually. For the moment, I enjoyed how he huffed in frustration when his sugar mama sent him to play in the corner. Left alone, Cynthia set about inspecting me with more leisure, as though admiring a dress in a shop window.

"Exactly how did you do it?"

I quirked an eyebrow. "Do what?"

She rolled her eyes. "Get the werewolf to become so obsessed with you? I thought wolves mate for life, and I don't see anything about you that would lead a bonded male to turn his back on his mate."

"Well, Cindy Loo-Who, that could be because your assumptions are wrong. Tobias isn't mated yet." I found myself giving up information without a second thought, the hurt and bitter truth of it still serving as a poison to loosen my care. "Besides, he doesn't care a lick about me. He's just a wolf at the end of his rope. He only reached out to me because he's pulling at strings."

"And that's why he twice defended you against one of my children?"

A ringing abounded in my ears. "Your children?"

"Oh, come on, Geri. Haven't you figured it out? When you asked which crèches are in the area, I convinced you not to bother. Didn't it occur to you I did that because I had something to hide?"

"Wait, so you're telling me that…" My mouth went dry, my mind raced to piece together the clues. "*You* sent Donovan."

Cynthia nodded. "Yes, and thank you so much for taking care of him for me. He was *such* a disappointment. I told Kai that, but I'm afraid my Hawaiian son is a bad judge of character. I've sent him on a mission to find a replacement now. Luckily, he's decided to scout at

Northwestern instead of WCU. In the meantime, I got to see if the werewolf intervening in your fight was just a fluke, or if there was really something going on. And lucky me, the moment you were in mortal danger, Mr. Furry showed up. Want to tell me again there's nothing between you two?"

"There's nothing," I assured her. "I can't stand Tobias. I've been trying to get him to leave for months."

"Too bad he didn't listen. Since he stayed, however, I'll make use of him. Just as I'll do with you."

"Me?" I asked. "What possible use could you have for me?"

"I don't mind getting blood on my hands, when the time comes for the wolves to die. But why should I, when I have a wolf-slayer at my disposal?"

I barely contained my laughter. A glow grew in Cynthia's cheek, as though she still had the power to blush.

"What's so funny, hood?"

"Just that, you think it's possible for me to kill a werewolf," I said. "I haven't taken my rites yet. I couldn't kill a wolf any more than Jess could. Besides, what could you and Karmarov want to learn from the wolves that isn't already known?"

Cynthia jerked her head back and cackled. "Karmarov? My dear, he's a hopeless, idealistic academic. Igor's gone soft in the tooth. I'm just making use of this fabulous facility he has access to. I'm afraid what I'm after has very pragmatic intentions."

"Yeah, like what?"

A maniacal grin stretched across her face. "I'm going to decimate the wild wolves, just like we did the slayers. And when they're all gone, there'll be no one who can stop us. Say you can't take on a wolf? Fine, I'm sure I can derive other projects where having a hood at my disposal will prove useful. Settle in, Gerwalta Kline. You could be here a while."

TWENTY-THREE

Hours must have passed, but how many, I couldn't know for sure. Even denied a way to see outside, I sensed dawn inherently, followed by the pull of the sun across the horizon and the late afternoon rise of the moon, and again, sunset. Had Amy noticed I never came home? How long would it take before my non-presence alerted her there was something wrong? And when she started to ask questions, would Cynthia send out a vamp with a little more tact and success to derail her curiosity? Somehow, I had to get out of here before that happened. But more importantly, with the full moon approaching, I had to get out of here before Tobias and his fiancée lost any hope of avoiding moon madness. How I was going to achieve: one, breaking myself out; two, breaking out two wolves being held prisoner by up to three vampires and a partial slayer with unknown abilities; three, getting them back to their packs half a world away before the full moon; and four, keeping my roommate both safe and ignorant of all the above, I hadn't the foggiest.

Halfway through the day, I awoke from a dreamless sleep to find a cloth sack on the floor next to me. In it, a water bottle, some fruit, cheese, and bread. I took a few sips of the water, and set the rest aside. I wasn't about to eat anything Cynthia and Jess gave me. Besides, I had gone through several training exercises that forced me to endure without resources for up to a week. Going twenty-four hours without grub wasn't about to do much to me. Other needs, however, didn't respond to willpower as well.

"Unless you expect me to designate a corner for you to hose down once a day, I could really use a potty break," I called out to the void.

At first, I thought my words may have gone unheard. A few minutes later, however, the good old professor himself came into view.

"I'm really very sorry about this, Miss Kline," Karmarov said, his words soft, his gaze tender. "I never intended for you to become one of Cynthia's subjects."

I kept my eyes trained on him, emotionless, giving him not the slightest satisfaction to see how betrayed I felt at having trusted him. "You know, something you said to me once makes a lot more sense now, about how some of your kind with a lot of power hide in plain sight? Which leads me to wonder, who exactly is Cynthia?"

"A vampire whose confidence I'm not interested in losing," was all he said. "If you need to use the facilities, I'd be happy to accompany you."

"I haven't needed to be accompanied to the bathroom since I was three."

Apples blossomed in his cheeks. "Of course, I wasn't suggesting that I would be in the restroom with you. I only meant that I would take you."

"I guess if you're my only choice, we just have to go with that, don't we? Now, how do I get out of here? I don't see any door."

No sooner had I asked the question than Karmarov squatted, taking on a frog pose one moment, and rocketing into the air the next. Getting over the twelve-foot wall presented as much of a challenge to him as stepping over a rain puddle. He landed just a foot from me without much of a sound, not even to my sensitive ears. I took a step back, reflexively feeling myself outmatched in his presence.

The professor held up his arms. "I'm not going to hurt you. I'm sorry to say this, but the only way for me to take you out of here is to carry you. The iguanas who were kept in this enclosure years ago didn't have much need of doors, and I'm afraid the ladders that used to allow the researchers access from the gangplank above have long since disappeared. So have many of the gangplanks."

I assumed zombie pose. "Fine, carry me then."

Karmarov blinked twice in quick succession. "Just like that, you trust me to be that close?"

"I don't trust you at all, but I know what my abilities are, and I know roughly what yours are. I'm a nascent hood. You're a centuries-old vampire. If you want to hurt me, I can't really stop you. Besides, my bladder is about to explode."

He took me in a you-Jane-me-Tarzan hold, all while wrinkling his nose. "I admit, one thing I do not miss about being mortal is the need for such indelicate functions.

Hold on, the g-forces involved in the leap are a little hard for a mortal to endure."

The hall that ran between the four different enclosures didn't give me much clue about how I could get out of here, or where Kara might be. Whitewashed cinderblocks gleamed under humming fluorescent lights. The scent of bleach stained the air. At the end of the corridor lay a windowless metal door.

"How does the university not know about all this?"

Karmarov's eyes roamed the edges of the room. "I've been able to make the records say the experiments carried on here during the war era have left the room unsafe for use. Hueys take every quarantine sign at face value."

When we reached the door, he swiveled in front of me, waiting, staring at me like he was studying my reaction to see if I appreciated the ugly brown paint that covered it.

"Nothing?"

Nothing what? What was he getting at? "Full bladder."

He tipped his head to the side. "Interesting. And if I open the door?"

The world shifted. A roil of my stomach only momentarily preceded a swirl in my head. My mind raced from annoyed curiosity to shocked understanding. There was no doubt, none whatsoever, that there was a wolf nearby. I'd known from Jess's loose lips that they hadn't gotten Tobias. What was Karmarov doing, pointing out to me that the English wolf was nearby? The sensation that tugged just below my belly button matched perfectly the effect he'd had on me the other times we'd been close. It had to be him.

Bracing me from behind, Karmarov pulled me over the threshold and into a vestibule with three doors: one to my left through which I could see a somewhat rust-dusted enamel sink and toilet, the one behind me we had just passed through, and another to my right, an unremarkable wooden door like any in the Browning Building above.

"I'll give you two minutes," the professor said, pushing me through the door on my left. "Use it wisely."

Even though my mind raced with the overload of thoughts, I still needed to attend to biological needs. That effort addressed, however, I knew exactly what Karmarov wanted me to do. The only question was why. He obviously wasn't about to rebel and act out against Cynthia and Jess on my behalf. What, then, was his end game?

But I couldn't think about that now. I only had forty-five seconds, tops, to do what needed to be done. I pulled in a breath, slow and steady, through my nose, and exhaled a deep sigh through my mouth. In the cracked mirror over the sink, my eyes brightened, a tinge of silver lining my brown irises, as I called on my innate abilities. I pushed my senses out, taking in the size and shape of everything around me. Inside my chest, a warmness formed.

Please, Tobias, I don't know if this will work, but if you sense my proximity, move toward it. I'm here. I'm here, and I think Kara is too.

Pounding on the door made my heart race. Looking down, I realized my hands had been under the ice-cold running water as my mind drifted. I reached up and turned off the faucet.

"Sorry, just washing up."

Karmarov gave me an expectant look as he opened the door and ushered me out. "Did you take care of what you needed to do?"

"Yeah, I think so."

"Good," he said, motioning back towards the heavy metal door. The painted *silver-plated* door, through which I'd never be able to sense a wolf. "I want you to know, Miss Kline, that no matter what Cynthia says, I didn't lie to you. I really am trying to find a way to restore the slayers. Unfortunately, Cynthia's research is the one that is getting all the attention in our little community right now. Genetics is all the rage, even among vampires."

"Trying to make sure all vamps have blue eyes and blonde hair, or whatever characteristics it is you consider preferable?"

"As you are a red hood descended from Germanic bloodlines, I can't help but take some amusement at your statement." Karmarov again took me up in his arms, preparing to jump. "What is the number one problem werewolves face?"

"Besides my mother?" I deadpanned.

"Diversity, Miss Kline," he said, ignoring my quip and taking another effortless stride through the air. It was easy to imagine why peasants of old thought vampires could fly. The way they defied gravity would certainly leave one with that impression.

"It's ironic that while our population is exploding beyond the capacity of city centers to support it undetected, werewolves are becoming more and more isolated. Destruction of habitat affects them the same way it effects any species."

Reflex pushed me to counter, to tell him about the matrons' database for tracking the packs, before thinking better of it. Karmarov might be playing things down the middle, or he might just be acting the friend to see if he could find out what I'd already stupidly told to Jess. Instead, I thought about Tobias, about how he'd mentioned the clutch that moved into his region when a nearby city had grown large enough to sustain it, leaving the packs that lived on the town's edge antsy.

Karmarov set me down gently, giving me enough space to feel somewhat, if foolishly, at ease as he continued.

"And yet, in this information age, where our *virtual* boundaries have all but disappeared, we're even more in danger. Supes have become overly cautious about reaching out to other communities, not sure who to trust. One cannot blame them, I suppose, but it does have effects. Their gene pool is narrowing. Packs that have exchanged mates for centuries now are pushed further from each other, and we all know how werewolves disdain long-distance travel."

"But I've never heard anyone mention anything about the packs being in danger due to lack of genetic diversity. If that was an issue, don't you think I'd have heard?"

Karmarov grinned, as though letting me in on a secret. "So you're suggesting someone is keeping that information contained? If one were to entertain the idea that such a thing might be happening, then one would have to ask himself – or *herself* – who would have such power, and more importantly, the motivation to keep such knowledge private.”

I didn't have to ponder that beyond two quick blinks to know the who. The Matrons were the only ones with unfettered access to the database our kind had spent the last few decades developing, who communicated openly and frequently through clandestine means about their local issues. They claimed it was to help wolves find mates across packs: an excuse I'd never bought. But was this it? Was my mother and her ilk actually trying to solve a problem among the wolves no one had yet admitted aloud? If so, then why keep it secret? The answer to that kept itself hidden in the details.

“Are you familiar with animal husbandry, Miss Kline?”

I shook my head. “I'm not from the part of Michigan with farms and feed lots. We're copper and timber in the U.P.”

“But surely you must understand how some farmers… even dog breeders, will go to great lengths to control mating and produce the ideal stock.” Karmarov turned, eyeballing the top of the holding cell. “Of course, wolves have natures which won't allow for trading out partners once a mating occurs. You are aware of the bond that werewolf couples experience, are you not?”

I swallowed. Hard. “Firsthand.”

If he recognized the pain in my throat and the crack in my voice, he made no acknowledgment. Instead, he leapt, landing just on the outside of my pen. Karmarov turned back to me, pushing his hand to the glass.

"Control is about more than doing, Gerwalta. It's also about undoing. Think about that." Then his hand dropped away. "If you need to use the facilities again, just call. I can come down from my office at any point tonight. Cynthia and Jess are otherwise occupied."

TWENTY-FOUR

Towards dawn, Karmarov brought me more food.

"I need to use the bathroom again."

I couldn't be sure of the meaning of the smile that blipped across his face before disappearing. "Of course."

Once in the small lavatory again, I was hit with the same awareness as before. Somewhere very nearby there was a werewolf. This time when I emerged, instead of striking up a conversation with me, Karmarov took me through the third door, to a small room, on the wall of which were several lever-handled silver doors.

I was standing inside a morgue. Or at least, what had been a morgue. The outdated décor suggested the room hadn't been refurbished for some time. Yet, the level of cleanliness, right down to the subtle scents of bleach and formaldehyde, suggested it had undergone some recent upkeep.

Cynthia stood at the back, clicking her fingernails on one of the refrigerator doors.

"What do you feel right now, hood?"

If she thought I was going to cooperate, she had another thing coming. I bit my tongue, crossed my arms, and smirked.

"Fine, be that way."

Her nail-polished fingers wrapped around the lever of the unit and pulled up. When the door opened, a sheen of condensation wafted out, dissipating just inches from the rim and replaced by a gentle flow of mist. Ball bearings whirred as Cynthia reached in and pulled out the slab, on which the man's body lay. Without any clothing and covered up to his chest by a white sheet, I couldn't gather too much about him, other than the obvious that he had been stout and built when he'd been alive.

"Anything now?" Cynthia raised an eyebrow.

"Don't know what you're expecting," I said. "I guess I'm vaguely curious why you have an autopsied body in the basement?"

Cynthia blinked. "His name was Nick Somfield, and he was an alpha."

And with that, I suddenly felt too many things. Sadness, disappointment, regret, anger, confusion. She wanted a reaction, she got a reaction. My fist convulsing, I practically growled my answer. "Tobias's brother. You murdered him."

A corner of Cynthia's mouth rose. "Nonsense, Geri. I harvested him for study, the way one does with any animal. I'm going to assume, then, that you had no idea what this man was until you learned *who* he was. How delightful to hear! Igor, bring her along."

In a few swift moves, the body of Tobias's brother disappeared into the cooler as Karmarov nudged me out of the room and up the hallway. When we stopped abruptly, it was before a holding cell not so different from the one in which I'd been, with one big exception: it had a door, one on which the lock was molded in silver.

Only one kind of prisoner would need such a pricey precious metal.

She must have been a true sight to behold before her captivity. Echoes of beauty still traced the edges of her face. Dressed in ragged clothes more ripped than whole, I wondered how many times she had put herself through the rigors of a transformation. That she had tried to get out in her wolf form was evident; the cinderblock wall at the back of the cell bore a number of claw marks. I had no doubt about who the woman with dull mocha skin and a frizz of matted, unkempt hair was. Only, it didn't make sense. She was a mere dozen feet from me, but I couldn't pick up any sense of her at all, not the way I did with the other wolves. I was blind to her lycanthropic nature.

But that wasn't what really concerned me. What did concern me was how a supernatural being could look so haggard. How little had they fed her for her body to waste away like this? How little did they care for her?

I lashed my head to the side, fury erupting in my voice. "What kind of monster are you?"

"The kind that always gets her way." Cynthia's smile beamed. "But for what it's worth, I can say that we are not entirely to blame for her state. No, not entirely. Kara's been offered a diet from hamburgers to raw lamb. I even had some human flesh given to her, just in case she was a wolf who enjoyed that kind of thing. She barely eats or drinks. She spends her days sleeping, and her nights when we aren't running tests on her howling. She used to take on her wolf every night. Now, I think she's lost interest in it."

I ground my teeth. "She hasn't lost interest. She's losing control. She's on the edge of lunacity. She's probably scared to take her wolf at this point. She may not be able to find her way back."

Cynthia laid a finger on her chin and tilted her head. "I've always wondered why the werewolves were so resistant to being their stronger selves."

"You really don't get it, do you?" I pointed at the poor woman beyond the glass, who so far hadn't even been able to move her head to look at me. "This *is* her stronger self. She's on edge of losing her control, but she's holding it in. You have no idea how hard that is for her."

"Such humanistic sentimentality. But then, I wouldn't expect a *nascent* hood, to understand what true power is. You've never felt it."

"I have, the moment I turned my back on my mother and refused to become the weapon she wanted me to be."

"A hood?"

The whisper came from within. Both Cynthia and I turned, taking in Kara's desperation with surprise.

Cynthia stepped back, pointing at me. "Not just any hood. She's the Red Matron's only daughter. Are you quaking in your boots, Kara?"

The she-wolf's head fell, her eyes growing distant and her voice small. "I fear nothing now, except the moon."

Cynthia turned back to me, rolling her eyes and waving her hand. "She's been saying that for days. I don't know what she means."

Did vamps really not get moon madness? If Cynthia didn't know, I wasn't about to tell her. Luckily for me, Cynthia didn't even inquire. Instead, she asked me the question I had been dreading.

"Now, what I want to know from you is, can you sense her?"

I swallowed down my nerves, kept my pulse steady. "No, I can't."

The vampire actually clapped and jumped, looking so much closer to her physical age than her actual one. Even Karmarov, standing just beyond us, seemed taken aback by Cynthia's sudden childishness.

"You've made me very happy, Geri. That's exactly what I wanted to hear." Her head jerked to the side. "Okay, Igor, put her in now."

"What? Wait, no!"

Normally, going into a room with a werewolf would be no problem. But this wasn't normal. The she-wolf had obviously been put through hell, and was on the edge of losing herself. On top of that, if her pack had the same adversarial relationship with hoods, leaving her as spiteful and vindictive as Tobias, she wasn't exactly going to suggest I pull up a chair and have a cup of tea.

Karmarov's touch could have been rougher. As manhandling went, his was civil. Nevertheless, as he undid the silver locks and corralled me through the door, I couldn't ignore the fact that he was shoving me into a room with a nearly feral fucking werewolf. Moments before I passed through, however, he pulled me close, putting his mouth to my ear.

"You're going to need every bit of your abilities to get out of this one, Geri."

Great, so he was going to both imprison me with my eternal foe and taunt my total lack of uber magical skills. Perhaps he'd also like to give me a papercut and pour lemon juice all over it.

Not knowing what else I could threaten him with, I hit him in the only way I could think. "You're never going to get tenure like this!"

Next thing I knew, I lay prostrated on a cold, misty floor. I looked back over my shoulder just in time to see Karmarov turn the lock again, before he and Cynthia slinked away. No need to stand around to see how this went down; a camera was mounted on a tripod in the identical cell across the hall, its lens turned directly on us.

The most important thing: not to panic. Panic was born of assumptions. I couldn't assume that Kara was about to leap up and shred me limb from limb, even though the over-under on that was a thin line requiring a microscope to see.

Backing myself to against a wall, I sat, noting how her head hadn't moved at all. Was she trying to ignore me, or honestly indifferent to my presence? It didn't matter. The only way I could see to gain a foothold in this situation was to engage her in conversation, and hope I could pull out the strength of her humanity by making it her focus.

"I'm Geri… *Gerwalta* Kline."

"The daughter of Red Matron." Kara's lips barely moved. "About time the hoods became involved. Red

Matron might be the only one strong enough to defeat a vampire."

"Actually, she doesn't know. Only I do."

"Then I am doomed."

Forgetting all caution, ignoring all instinct, I rushed to Kara's side, laying a hand on her shoulder. "No, you're not."

"And just who is going to save me, hood. You?" Finally, she looked at me, and I immediately wished she hadn't. Her bloodshot eyes barely reflected light, and the bags under her eyes and purple patches on her cheeks told me she'd been physically roughed up as well as mentally imprisoned. That, or she'd injured herself thrashing around, trying to force her body from one form to the other.

I wanted to ask how long she'd been here, but I already knew the answer to that. The variable wouldn't be measured in the number of days, weeks, or months, but in the simple fact that however long it was, had been too long.

"I'm only a nascent," I admitted. My own words sounded like a rationalization, like an excuse. Like an apology.

"Of course you are. Why wouldn't you be?"

"Do you, um, mind if I ask you something?" Purely a rhetorical lead. "Do you know why you're here? What are they trying to accomplish with you? Why are the vamps after the wolves?"

"Isn't it obvious? Because we have the ability to fight them. Assuming they don't gang up on us when we're driving along a country road one night." Her head shook, as though freeing herself from the belief. "Five of them ganged up on me. I was on my way to see my boyfriend. They ran me off the road, then bound me with silver chains. Two days later, I was here."

"And you've been here ever since?"

Her face soured. "You think they let me traipse about the city on weekends do you?"

"No, I just…" It was going to sound crazy to her, I knew it would. "I can't sense you. You're different somehow."

"Am I? It wouldn't surprise me." Her chest shook with silent sighs. "So many things they've done to me. I don't know them all. When life had mercy, I was not awake. And when it didn't…"

"I'm so sorry, Kara." As tears pricked the edges of her eyes, I knew I needed to keep her focused. As loose a grip as she had on controlling her form, becoming overly emotional could trigger a change. I had no silver, and no ability to access a full hood's strength. If she changed, I was dead. If I died, so would she. "You said you were on your way to meet your boyfriend? Is that all he is, really? Because the way Tobias tells it, you and he are practically mated already."

With that single name, her face brightened. "Tobias? How, how is that possible?"

"He's in Chicago looking for you." I pulled away, if only to give her a moment to adjust to that fact without any distraction. "He's been trying to convince me that you were in Browning this whole time, but I didn't believe him. I'm in this building most days of the week, and I never got a blip from you."

The brow of Kara's forehead creased. "What a barmy! If he's been here the whole time, he's just as close to going over the edge as I am. Stupid, dumb dog."

"Actually, Kara, I think he might be our way out of here."

She lifted an eyebrow. "There is no way out of here."

"I think there might be. Only, we have to wait for daybreak when the vamps are asleep."

TWENTY-FIVE

I didn't know if it was desperation, an inability to concentrate on anything but her sanity, or just a total lack of credulity led Kara not to argue. A few hours after I'd been placed in her cage, Cynthia and Karmarov sauntered by, on their way to their day rest, with Jess close on their heels like the little sissy sycophant thrall he was.

Cynthia glared at us, disappointed. "She's still alive."

I didn't bother to ask which of our continued existences pissed her off most. Kara, as when I first entered, stayed seated on her folding chair, motionless except for the slow rise and fall of her shoulders as she breathed. I remained in the corner of the cell, searching for a comfortable sleeping position.

"We'll use it to our advantage then." Cynthia turned over her shoulder to Jess. "I want to see what happens when the full moon rises and Kara takes on her wolf. For that to happen, they both need to survive the day."

I raised my voice, flustering them to be reminded I could speak. "Just put me back where I was before. It would be hard for even the most determined werewolf to get to me through a silver-plated wall."

Amused, Cynthia nodded at me approvingly. "You've figured out our little design secret, have you?"

"Yeah, but I'm not really sure what you hoped to achieve. Whatever you did to the stiff you got in the morgue and this wolf, I can't sense them. You've…masked them somehow."

"And just what makes you think that those are the only wolves we've had down here since you've been on campus?" She leaned over, putting her hands on her knees. "Where do you think all those little samples in the silver box upstairs came from?"

Then, turning back to Jess, she said, "Careful with the hood. They're trained to use anything and everything as a weapon."

Jess bobbed his head. "What do I do if they go after each other?"

"Then make sure you are recording. We should still learn enough from the brawl to know if Igor's chasing ghosts."

The professor's back went rigid, his fists balling. His serene voice belied obvious frustration. "I've been studying blood and tissue samples since the invention of the microscope. DNA samples since the technology came along to make it possible. I know what I saw, Cynthia. I'm not wrong about her."

"And yet, the wolf lives." Evil manifested as a grin on Cynthia's face. "At least for now. When the full moon comes up tonight, we'll see if your theory holds any water."

"It will hold the ocean," Karmarov assured her. "But I stress again, there are other ways to go about this. Ones that don't risk Gerwalta losing a limb, or worse, her life."

"A deal is a deal, Igor. I promised that if she survives, she's your guinea pig. I didn't promise you'd get all her associated limbs in the process."

For the first time since I'd met him, I saw anger take hold of Igor Karmarov. His fangs lowered in a second. That single alteration, combined with the narrowed eyes, bowed head, and creased forehead, let one see that, while subservient, the old vampire was not some domesticated beast that Cynthia could dismiss at will.

"What good is she to me if she's rendered incapable of fighting?"

"What does that matter to me?" Cynthia twirled a hand through the air. "Besides, I thought you only wanted to study her genetic makeup. Wouldn't that be more efficient if you only had to cart her arm or leg around from place to place, and not have to worry about feeding it, washing it, taking it to go potty?"

"Understanding why she is the way she is at a genetic level is only part of my query. I also have to see how that genetic uniqueness…"

"Blah, blah, blah." Cutting him off, Cynthia raised her hand to her mouth, slowly working her jaw through a languid yawn. "I've heard it before. Don't worry. I'm sure we'll wake up tonight and find your precious hood still intact. Jess, remember: any changes, wake us. We might be a little slower than usual during the day, but we can still take care of a weakened werewolf and a nascent hood."

The two vampires continued past our cell, heading up the hall, beyond my vision. Jess, however, lingered, taunting me with his glare. He pointed to the camera mounted outside and pointed at our cell.

"If you decide to try to kill each other, at least try to make it look sexy."

Even distant Kara growled at that one. Jess squared her in his gaze, then licked his lips, before slithering out of sight.

The werewolf turned her weary head my way. "Now what?"

I settled myself back in the corner, using it to support myself in a sitting position and leaning my head to the side.

"Now, we sleep a little. We'll need strength tonight."

"I'm afraid that, if I sleep, I will never wake again to see the world through human eyes."

"You will, Kara. I promise. Try to get some rest. I can't do this alone."

TWENTY-SIX

When I awoke a few hours later, lying on the floor, I found myself surrounded by fur. Confused, I rubbed the sleep from my eyes and pulled myself up to sit. Beside me, a white belly of fur served as my pillow. My eyes went to the chair where Kara had been sitting when I'd fallen asleep. Nothing there, except a few scraps of cloth that no doubt had been the threadbare clothes she'd been wearing before.

Kara raised her snow-white snout. The fur over and leading up to her eyes abruptly turned gray with specks of red. Silver and black fur rimmed her neck like a scarf. Despite the thickness of her coat – typical for wolves from northern environs, though I suspected some of her lineage came from North Africa due to her human form – it didn't hide the fact that her skin hung loose about her, as though someone had deflated a wolf-balloon, leaving just enough helium for it to skirt the floor.

It wasn't night yet, so she must have taken her wolf deliberately.

"Can you change back?"

A thin, hollow whine answered me. She looked toward the camera trained on us both, then back to me.

"Ah, you don't think you should. Got it."

Her head tilted to the side, the wolf version of "what are you doing?"

"You ready?"

A weak yelp.

"Good. I'm going to get Jess to take me to use the bathroom. When he brings me back, be ready to act."

My whole body shook as I took to my feet and bounced in the direct line of the camera. If jumping around like a stranded person on a desert island at a passing boat didn't get Jess's attention, I wasn't sure what I would do.

"See someone you know, Geri?" he ground out when he came into view.

I avoided his jibe and stuck with the plan. "I need to use the bathroom."

Jess lifted a finger and pointed to the corner behind me. "Go ahead."

"Seriously? You can't expect me to just sit around in my own pee. Besides…" Jerking my head back toward the she-wolf, I drew his attention to the obvious. "…probably not a good idea if I go about 'marking territory' in a cell with a werewolf on the edge of going moon mad."

With a slanted eyebrow, he weighed my claim against his limited knowledge of werewolf behavior. "Is that true?"

"You've seen a dog lift its leg on every third tree, haven't you? Don't give werewolves too much credit just because they can take on a human form. In their heads, they're more mutts than men. Come on, Jess. I've really got to go."

The stoniness of his face began to show cracks. "Can't you just hold it? It's almost dark. The vamps will be back soon."

"You know the saying, when you got to go… Come on, my bladder is about to burst."

A tiny twitch, then a sigh, and finally Jess slipped his hand into his pocket, pulling out a key. He slipped it into the lock, but paused to point at Kara before turning the silver deadbolt.

"You show a single canine, you'll regret it. I got silver oxide spray, and I'm not afraid to use it." He dropped his hand to pull a small container out of his pocket, holding it next to the deadbolt like he was positioning a gun to dissuade a prisoner from charging.

If he thought a diluted mist of Ag_2O was about to stop a full-sized, mature she-wolf just hours away from full moon, he was a few trees short of a forest. Still, I wasn't about to clear him of his delusions.

"Listen to him, Kara. No reason for you to get hurt just because of my human biology. Okay?"

The wolf picked up on the cue, and yelped her acknowledgment.

Jess wasted no time in scooting me up the hall once I was out of the cell. He probably didn't suspect I was taking notes of every little move he made. The smallest part of winning a battle relied on muscle; both my parents had taught me early that my brain counted as my greatest weapon.

In the back of my mind, I began to index his behaviors and assets. Silver oxide spray: right pants pocket. Key to Kara's cell: left pants pocket. Being that he was right-handed, that made sense. It was a mistake, however, as silver oxide wouldn't deter me in the slightest. I was a hood; silver was my friend. I might not be able to command it yet, but he'd have better luck trying to douse me with seltzer water.

His left side, his weaker side, became my target. He'd try to either kick or hit me with a left, bringing it – and the key – closer.

"Because we never got a chance to talk after I knocked you out, let me make one thing clear," Jess said as he pushed me toward the bathroom. "Every minute I spent with you was torture. I belong to Cynthia."

"Yeah, I know how that whole thrall thing works. Sounds like she's in your head, nice and deep. Funny thing about that is, you don't realize what it means."

Let it fester. Let him try to figure it out.

Jess huffed. "What's that supposed to mean?"

At the bathroom, I turned back around. "Nothing, it's just… Vampires weren't the subject of my training, so I could just be wrong. But, as far as balances go, seems like, to have an equal playing ground, a slayer wouldn't be able to be put under thrall. If you are part-slayer, the genes must be recessive in you. I highly doubt anything Cynthia and Karmarov come up with in their research will ever work to awaken those properties in you."

I paused, turning around and leaning against the frame of the door coquettishly.

The seeds of doubt began to germinate. "What do you mean, if I'm part-slayer? Of course I'm part-slayer."

"I'm not saying you aren't. I'm just saying you're probably not slayer *enough* to be useful to them. You're just convenient. And if there's one thing I know about vampires, the second you stop being useful to them, then bam! They wipe your memory clean and send you off." I pressed a finger to my chin, feigning deep thought. "I wonder what cover story they'll come up with? Car accident that left you with amnesia? Experimental drug that fried your brain? Rare genetic condition that led to big gaps in your memory? Yes, that's it. That would fit in with the fact that you've been receiving payment for working in the lab of a geneticist."

"You have a creative imagination, Geri, I'll give you that."

"It's too bad we didn't get a little more time before Tobias showed up. I could have shown you just how creative I can be."

"You?" The word came out as an airy chuckle. "A virgin?"

Sticking out my chest to offer up what my cousin Markus mockingly called my "hood goods," I lowered my gaze, putting on the schmaltz. "Only technically. Remember, I dated a werewolf for two years. Just because we successfully kept ourselves from going all the way doesn't mean we didn't find ways to have a hell of a time. I have a catalog of skills that don't require a full immersion."

"And am I supposed to believe that you want to share these skills with me, even though it turns out I'm one of the bad guys?"

A shrug, one with my left shoulder a little higher than the other, reached Jess on a purely subconscious level. Animal instinct drove the predator to square an attack on the weaker side. The side where the muscles didn't show as much strength. With a devious smirk on his face, Jess raised his left arm, using it to ballast himself against the wall as he leaned toward me. When his mouth began to angle toward mine and his eyes closed, I wondered what lottery I had won to have him fall into my trap so easily. Just as I was about to wrap my hands around his waist and distract him with a kiss, however, he paused.

Jess's eyes flew open. "You think this is working?"

With a vigorous yank on my right side, I fell down into the bathroom. Cold tiles under flat palms, I pivoted from the heap I'd landed in on the floor and looked up at the dominating figure before me. Jess, both hands balled on his hips, sneered at me.

"Like I said, I'm Cynthia's." He pointed to the porcelain pot at the edge of the tiny loo. "Do your business, and get on with it."

The moment the door was closed, I leapt to my feet and stuffed the key into my bra. I had to be quick. Making a show of using the bathroom, I turned on the faucet labeled "C," closed my eyes, and centered my mind, pulling on all the nascent power in my body, and hoping Tobias hadn't given up, that he was still close enough.

How stupid of them to somehow put a silver coating around the holding pens, but not the bathroom. It was like giving me a periscope to see into the world above the surface. At first, I wasn't sure if the niggle poking at the edge of my nervous system meant he was close, or if the consequences of limited food and water had begun to have an effect. After one more deep breath, the sensation sharpened and normalized, then, heightened. Tobias – at least, I'd assume it was him, since I didn't know of another werewolf in Chicago – drew near. My senses flooded with awareness of his proximity. I felt the corners of my mouth dance, even as I remembered my mother's words.

You're only a nascent, and the wolves find themselves drawn to you. When you complete your rites and walk through the Gates of Fire, they will not be able to resist. You'll be able to lure them away from anyone, to anywhere. You'll never have to chase a wolf the way the rest of us do. When you want, the wolves will come to you.

A pounding rhythm on the door brought me back to the here and now.

"Time's up!" Jess bellowed, then rapped the door again.

My eyes flew open, broken from my reverie, to find myself staring at the mirror. My eyes glowed, the typical rim of light blue outlining my irises. If I could will it away, I would. There would be no hiding it from Jess once the door opened, and backed into a small room without a weapon, he'd have the advantage in any sort of attack.

Something must be usable as a weapon. With a single sweep from left to right, I cataloged the bathroom. Its Spartan design didn't offer much possibility, not even a plunger next to the toilet I could use as an impromptu bat or bar of soap on the sink to throw as a distraction.

The only available item: a thinned roll of toilet paper on the back of the toilet.

Wait a minute – the toilet!

In a blinding moment of inspiration, I had my plan. I dropped to my knees, hugged the toilet, and did the best impression of vomiting I could manage.

"Jesus Christ!"

Three steps took Jess across the length of the bathroom. The moment I sensed him leaning down to inspect me, I acted.

Gripping the edges of the toilet seat, I yanked with all my strength. The porcelain lid separated with a crack, flying through the air and catching Jess under the chin, sending him reeling back and flattening against the wall. Had I been stronger, he may have gone out with one blow. No such luck.

He stumbled to his feet, dazed but dangerous. "You're going to pay for that one, Geri."

Teeth gnashing, I said, "Bill me."

He charged again, but it was opening night in the Gerwalta-will-not-go-down-easily Season, and I was ready. Faking a blow coming down on his right, Jess's arms went up to block me. I pulled back, but the distraction was just long enough for me to swing a kick right to his groin.

Doubled over, the so-called semi-slayer was all too easy to pick off. A hard conk with the rim of the toilet seat to the back of his head, and he was out. Jess's body slumped, his head landing under the sink and his face flat against the floor.

I didn't know if he was actually part-slayer, or if that had been a lie Cynthia told to manipulate him. If he was, he might, like hoods, heal more quickly than humans. The last thing I wanted was for Kara to be stolen of her already-limited strength by the silver oxide spray he carried. I reached into Jess's pocket, pulling out the miniature bottle, before emptying it into the toilet and flushing. As I shoved it back into his pocket (nothing like a false sense of security to distract a foe), the now-empty bottle pinged when it hit something.

Reaching in, something palm-sized, plastic, thin, and rectangular filled my hands. Jess's student ID? Of all the things to carry around in his pocket in Cynthia's dungeon, why that? Was there a secret student café I hadn't yet discovered in Browning's basement as well?

I stepped over his body and ran out in the hall, down to Kara's cell. She found life when I shoved the key in the lock and opened the door.

"Come on, I don't know how long he'll be out for, and the sun is already setting."

Kara yelped, rushing through the door as soon as the crack allowed for it. I dove back in only long enough to grab the dress that still sat on the chair. It may be torn and dirty, but it would have to do for the moment. Together, we hightailed it up the hall, in the direction we had seen the vampires running. After a few more similarly designed cells on either side, we came to an elevator lobby. Instead of call buttons, only a small, plastic opaque inset appeared next to the doors.

We looked at each other with equal confusion: me, gawking; Kara, tilting her wolf head.

Could it be so simple?

I reached into my pants pocket, pulled out Jess's card, and held it up to the black plastic inset on the wall. A beep preceded an electric hum, the sound of gears working and cables… cabling, as the elevator shaft shook gently.

Keeping my eyes glued to the doors, waiting for them to open and ready to attack anything and anyone that might be inside if needed, I said to Kara, "I know it's really close to sunset, and that even in your best condition, that would make it hard to change back to human, but can you?"

I'd seen wolf mannerisms all my life. I'd grown to be able to read their body language like a spoken tongue. Kara all but vocalized her question: Why?

I pointed at the elevator. "Tobias is near. I sensed his proximity. I… I actually was able to make him feel mine somehow, to like, call him here. I don't know how. Anyway, wherever this elevator opens, it's still going to be somewhere in Browning Hall. As soon as we find Tobias, I'll get both of you to my place before the sun sets; it's not too far away. But between here and there, you need to be human. We'll never be able to get away with two werewolves walking across campus. You may look a lot like huskies, but the fact that you're as big as miniature ponies won't go unnoticed."

Confusion, anticipation, trepidation… all passed in Kara's expression, until finally, she settled on determination. Gaining her paws, the wolf arched her back. Gray fur became consumed by a plane of mocha flesh. Elbows and knees took shape. A maw shrank back, morphing into a mouth and button nose. Soon, where there had been a canine stood the emaciated frame of the she-wolf in her human form.

Kara took to her feet and held out a hand for her dress. Like me, she had long ago let go any awkwardness at being nude.

"But what will happen when we get to your apartment and the moon rises?" she asked, slipping her clothes over her head. "And how will we get back to our packs before the moon sets? England is six hours ahead of Chicago. There's no way for us to travel that far in that amount of time."

"Maybe it won't be necessary? After all, you slipped into being human easily enough just now. Which was… really impressive, by the way, given how weak you are."

"I am beaten, but I'm still a beta." With a mournful huff, Kara shook her head. "*I* might be able to come back to flesh tomorrow morning, for one more night. But Tobias won't. If he left England the same time I was taken, he's on the edge of going mad."

"One thing at a time, Kara. First, we need to get out of here. I have a tranquilizer at my apartment. If you show signs you're out of control, I'll dose you. Don't worry about Tobias. I have a plan to help you both."

Her eyes went suddenly wet around the edges. "Why are you doing this? What kind of hood goes to such lengths to help wolves, ones that aren't from her territory at that?"

I didn't have time to answer her before the elevator stopped, and the doors opened up to an eerily familiar sight. Wire shelves and long gray boxes filled with slides. The air of the refrigerated room mixed with that of the elevator, forming a mist as chilled met warm. I led Kara, taking tentative steps, wondering how I had been in this room before and not noticed an elevator shaft.

As the doors closed behind us and I turned to see, I realized just how. Somehow the elevator bay had been disguised to look like a regular patch of wall.

Kara took a place beside me, gauging the scene with equal curiosity. "Why have an elevator hidden inside a deep freezer?"

"Because," I said, pointing at the door, "if it wasn't someone could look in here and see it. Karmarov's lab may have restricted entry, but it's still university property and must be accessible by some people on campus. Probably custodians and security, at least. But they didn't want anyone to know this was here. Karmarov himself said he fudged university records to make it look like nothing useful was still down here."

I shook out the confusion and refocused on both the plan, and the tingling in my fingers and chest that told me Tobias was near. So tingly, in fact, that I didn't doubt he was on the same floor with us. We just had to get out to find him. Hopefully Jess's student ID opened the main elevator down from the lab too, since as far as I knew, my ID was still in my bag back at the apartment.

Kara reached out to touch the door. Wisps of smoke wafted from her fingers the second her hand clasped the handle. She groaned, pulling back her scorched palm and holding it before her eyes, looking at her own hand as though it had betrayed her.

"Silver," I concluded. Now I realized why there were so many obvious layers of messy paint over the door. The whole thing must be made of it. Or at the very least, plated in it. "In case any of you escaped, a last measure to try to keep you in."

"Or one to try to keep others out," Kara said, dropping her head. She turned to me. "Do you still sense him being close?"

"Very close." I raised an eyebrow. "You can't?"

She shook her head, her gaze falling to the ground. "Whatever they've done to me, it had some effect. I couldn't sense what you were either when they brought you to me. Whatever the vamps are up to, they're putting us in serious danger. We need to know when an enemy approaches."

Catching my awkward pose, Kara shrugged.

"Sorry, no offense, but hoods where we come from aren't like you. They'd as soon chain us to a tree as look at us."

"The ones where I come from aren't much better."

I reached out, wrapping my hand around the handle of the door. Unlike Kara, I felt warmth, a sense of familiarity.

The silver wanted to speak to me, but I still did not know its language.

"Ready?"

The werewolf's chest rose and fell through a cycle of deep breaths. Finally, after a moment, she gave a jerky nod.

Neither of us could move the moment after we got through the door. What we were seeing was impossible.

Tobias, in the lab.

Bound in a silver cord, and standing between Prof. Karmarov and a very smug Cynthia, my silver blade at Tobias's throat.

TWENTY-SEVEN

"Kara, run!"

"Silence, dog!"

Cynthia yanked the silver cord, dragging Tobias closer.

Beside me, Kara whimpered. "You shouldn't have come. There's nothing you can do for me."

"Sounds like at least one of you understands the situation. Now…"

The Asian vampire pressed the blade to the werewolf's throat, drawing a pebble of blood. Air siphoned between Tobias's lower lip and teeth as he bit away his pain. The attempt to hide his suffering fell short; I had no doubt Kara understood her beloved's pain. Tears welled in the corner of his eyes.

"I will always come for you," he ground out. "I am thine, and thou art mine."

Cynthia ignored them, continuing to bark out ultimatums. "Let me make this really simple for you. Here's what's going to happen. The professor here is going to hit the lycanthropes with a heavy sedative. Geri, since it seems you've been able to outwit my thrall, you will go with Karmarov. He needs to do a few tests on you. Then, we're all going to take a little drive."

"Are you crazy?" I barked out. "They'll be moon mad by morning. They've been away from their packs for too long. They won't be able to change back to their human form."

"I don't really care." Cynthia shrugged. "Besides, this bitch isn't going to be useful to me for too much longer. I'm as likely to eat her as keep her come morning."

My nose wrinkled. "You're eating wolves?"

"Well, eating might be an overstatement. More like, drinking unto death."

Prof. Karmarov brought himself even with the other two. "If I can suggest, Miss Xin, sunset is minutes away. Handling the two werewolves will become exceedingly difficult after that. It may be wise for us to take action now, and deal in dialogue later."

"Not yet."

Cynthia handed off Tobias to Karmarov before sidling up to the she-wolf. Kara, chin stiff and teeth bared, let out a warning growl.

Cynthia's hands flew up in surrender. "Easy there, wolf, I only want to follow up on the line of questioning we've been going over the last few months." Pressing the blade to Kara's throat, she leaned in, whispering in her ear. "Now, who is the pretty boy who's crossed an ocean and stalked this side of Chicago for three months, looking for you?"

"Tobias Somfield."

"I knew that much from his immigration files, sweetie. Try again, and this time—" A bead of blood pearled where the tip of the blade punctured Kara's collarbone. "—tell me what I want to hear."

"He's my…" Kara bit back tears, bit back anger. "He's my mate."

I felt my world shift at the revelation. The next moment, I was struck dumb. Why would Tobias hide the fact that he was mated?

"How sad. That explains how he could follow us so easily. You are bonded – even though you've not officially been given permission by your alphas. You naughty, naughty wolf. But it's obvious he loves you. Look at him, traipsing about the city, looking for any clue to find you. He even buddied up to a hood, he was so determined. He wanted her to hunt you when he had failed. Do you love your mate, Kara?"

"Yeah," Kara sighed, her voice cracking. "I love him. Tobias, I love you."

The wolf finally showed signs of life, pulling at his restraints, trying to get closer. "You bloody vampire, stop! You've hurt her enough. Let her go!"

Cynthia stuck out her bottom lip. "Not nearly as much as you have, lover boy. Tell me, can you sense her? Just a few feet away from her, can you feel the pull all wolves feel when they are near their mates?"

This time, it was Tobias who lost all resolve from his features. Lowering his head, he shook it mournfully. "No."

"And yet, you made a pretty straight line for this lab when you came huffing and puffing in. If it wasn't the draw of your promised mate, then what exactly led you here?"

I went cold when, with anger in his eyes, Tobias snarled at me. "Somehow that hood keeps luring me to her whenever she's in danger. Evil cow, are you happy now? Now that you sprang this little trap and both Kara and I will die?"

"Okay, I seriously have no clue how you think I'm in on this," I replied. "FYI: I've been a prisoner here for the last two days."

I turned to Karmarov. "Why? What possible value is a nascent hood to you?"

Any compassion or collusion I may have thought I'd picked up on in the dungeon faded. The professor's monotonous tone showed no emotion.

"I have theories, but only theories. Is it just you, or all Reds who have your traits? I need further study. More test subjects."

"Further study? Why, you old…"

The room echoed back Kara and Tobias's groans. Inside myself, I felt the echo of the same force that pulled on them, forcing them into submission, robbing them of their humanity. I didn't need a mirror to see that my eyes glowed with the faint light of my power. Behind me Kara fell to all fours, her bones breaking, her skin prickling as hair follicles multiplied and bubbled. When changing at will, a wolf could mitigate the pain of a body remaking itself. When forced by the moon, the process was the worst kind of torture. At least, Cody had described it that way. I had no doubt now as I witnessed the moon-induced transformation with virgin eyes.

For the first time since Kara and I had emerged into the lab, the vampires showed their nerves. Karmarov dropped the silver thread that bound Tobias. The metallic twine pinged as it hit the floor, searing a path over the paws of the massive red and white-furred wolf. Cynthia stumbled backward, my silver blade falling from her grasp, as Kara's maw, still half-formed, chomped at her.

The vampires' only concern became the wolves. It should have been mine as well. A wolf under the pull of a full moon made for a foe even the bravest and strongest of hood matrons gave proper due. Having two, both more than likely doomed to be trapped in their lupine forms from moon madness, in a confined space? It wasn't a question of if I would get killed, it was a question of if my parents would be able to recognize my mangled corpse.

As metamorphized forms found balance on four legs, I dove for the silver blade. I didn't know what I could do, but I was useless without a weapon. The moment I had the blade in hand, my feet went out from under me. Before I could come to grips with the blurring scenery around me, I found myself upstairs in Karmarov's office, Karmarov standing next to me. I knew vampires were fast. I didn't know how fast.

I brandished the blade before me, a comic impression of a person who thought she stood a chance to calm the storm with a whisper. "Why?"

Shame filtered his eyes as he dipped his chin. "You are unique."

"How? Because I wanted nothing to do with this world?"

His hands threaded through my hair as snarls and groans, crashes and destruction, crawled up the winding staircase from the lab below.

"You can choose the type of person you want to be, Gerwalta Kline. Don't be the kind that runs away. You have to be in the game to change its outcome."

"So, what? You're helping me again? I'm dizzy at all your side-changing."

The professor became streaks before my eyes, moving with such velocity that I couldn't track him. In two blinks, he had crossed his office, opened a desk door, and sent his antique wooden office chair crashing against the wall, breaking it into several pieces in the process.

Karmarov rounded his desk to shove a handgun into my grasp. "Have you been trained in firearms?"

"I'm the daughter of the Red Matron. I've been trained in everything but compassion." I took note of the furry red-feathered dart in the loaded weapon. "Only one dart? But there are two wolves out there."

Karmarov turned. "I'm not giving it to you as a tactical weapon. It's for defense. The blast is strong enough to pierce a werewolf's hide, but it may take a few moments for the sedative to have an effect. Use whatever defensive maneuvers you've got hidden up your sleeve. You still have Jess's ID?"

I nodded, despite my confusion.

"Good," Karmarov said. "Make for the elevator. Sounds like both wolves are busy trying to take down Cynthia, but if your running triggers one of their instincts and it tries to attack, shoot it. You get out, no matter what, okay?"

"What? No way. I am not leaving Kara and Tobias behind so you two can throw them in a cell and use them as test monkeys."

Karmarov's patience began to fade. "Didn't you hear what Tobias said? He can't sense Kara. The experiment is over. We found a way to uncouple a werewolf bond."

Was I hearing what I really thought I was hearing? The vampires had discovered a way to undo the bond between mating wolves? Impossible. That bond glued packs together. Mates were so true to each other, adultery in the werewolf world had never been witnessed. Packs were family, an interconnected web of devoted pairs who'd fight to the death for each other and their progeny.

"But that would entirely alter the nature of the species."

"Correct," Karmarov confirmed. "Now you see why we have to stop this. If Cynthia survives this battle and she figures out that I let you get away on purpose, all my work will have been for nothing. Get out. I'll become smoke, go to the basement, and make sure Mr. Harmond's memories also conveniently disappear. If anyone asks you about me, you must never tell them I aided you, understand?"

Every new truth revealed twisted my old understandings into tighter knots. "Just whose side are you really on?"

"I'm on the side of life, Miss Kline." He winked at me. "Good luck, and until we see each other again."

My gaze shifted, from the open door on the far side of the room, to the empty office, and then to the weapon in my hand. My eyes fell on the splintered fragments of the wooden office chair, wondering how a creature who could cause such destruction without even intending it, could also show such tenderness for a few werewolves and a nascent hood.

And I wondered if he thought I was really going to do as he asked.

No matter what Karmarov said, I wasn't going to abandon the wolves. Even if it cost me my life, I wasn't about to be the kind of hood — I wasn't going to be the kind of *person* who cared more about saving her own skin than those in peril. Still, I was only a nascent, and two wolves on the edge of madness and under the pull of the full moon were just as likely to kill me as accept my aid.

Looking at the gun, I realized what I needed to do. Below, I'd only have one shot. I needed to make it count.

Before me was chaos made fur, fang, and flesh. The four workstations where a few days ago I had scanned slide after slide, oblivious to the dungeon and prisoner three floors below me, had been laid to waste. The tabletop machines lay in broken pieces on the floor. The assorted vials of solution and cleaners, pools of broken glass.

Amidst the chaos, Cynthia stood in the center of the room, acting like some sort of centrifuge that spun the wolves out every time they got within reach. Kara and Tobias took turns throwing their bodies full force, only to have them lashed in the corner. I lifted the tranq gun, fixed the vampire in my sight, and waited for the coast to be clear. Pressure built on the tip of my finger as I started to squeeze, but I stopped dead in my tracks when Cynthia caught me on the stairs. The momentary distraction was all Tobias needed to settle his teeth around Cynthia's wrist.

A terrifying screech emanated from the vampire's mouth as she flung her arm, taking the red wolf for a ride through the air. Drywall shattered as his body crashed. Kara, instead of repeating the pattern of fronting an attack against the vampire who had held her hostage for three months, sped to the side of her beloved.

In the act of turning her back on that same woman.

In a blur, Cynthia found her way to one of the workbenches left in disarray. The silver box that started my last few days of horror lay among the debris. Its hinges proved no obstacle; Cynthia merely grasped ahold of the box's lid by the edges and yanked, and it came off. With no more challenge than it would take me to fold a paper plate, so she too managed to contort the lid, rolling it, altering it, making it into a conic tube.

Cynthia raised the newly molded weapon over her head; I raised the gun.

The vampire brought her newly forged weapon down with a yowl.

Silent, the reluctant hood within me pulled the trigger and shot.

TWENTY-EIGHT

The doors of the elevator connected to the dungeon opened just as the she-wolf and female vampire became lifeless forms on the lab floor. Karmarov held a still unconscious Jess in his arms, as easily balanced as if he were carrying a stack of blankets. Confusion overtook him, his eyes narrowing.

"How?"

I held up the tranq gun as evidence. "I'm sorry, professor, I had to repurpose your chair. I replaced the dart with a piece of wood."

"You were supposed to use it against the wolves. Your job was to get away."

"No, my job was to protect the wolves. I'm a hood. That's what I'm supposed to do."

But his unspoken implication remained true. I hadn't protected the wolves. Kara's body lay in a red pool, which grew larger by the moment. I held my breath as Tobias's paws touched down in his mate's blood, sniffing at her neck. The she-wolf made no movement. I looked to Karmarov.

His expression drooped, confirming with a somber shake of his head what I feared true. "She's dead."

My legs felt leaden, the gravity of each step heavy, as though I was walking down into a dark destiny that would pull me under. "Tobias. Tobias, I'm so sorry. I– "

"Geri, stay back!"

But Karmarov should have saved his words for himself. The moment Tobias accepted that his mate was dead, his ire turned on the sole person left who had contributed to her imprisonment. Ice and fire shot up my spine, instinct telling me to defend. But who did I defend? The vampire who had lied to me, only to save me? The werewolf who had repeatedly saved me, but detested me?

Trepidation made Karmarov's movements deliberate. With exceeding care, he rotated, setting Jess on the floor. He put his hands up, backing away. The wolf held himself in parallel, a rumbling growl on the air. Teeth bared, Tobias assumed an attack posture, looking for just the right moment to spring.

"I understand your anger, Mr. Somfield, but please know, I'm on your side. I'm so sorry about Kara."

As though his daring to speak Kara's name was the only thing standing between Karmarov and her mate's rage, the werewolf pounced. Tobias pinned the vampire to the floor, becoming a torrent of teeth, fur, and revenge.

Across the room, rapid-fire quandary pelted my determination with conflict. Karmarov had helped me, but did that make him my friend? Tobias had saved me from death twice, but did that mean he'd hold back from killing me if I put myself between him and the vampire? No matter what the professor did for me tonight, the fact remained that he'd knowingly held a kidnapped woman in a dungeon for months while Cynthia performed who-knew-what diabolic experiments and rendered countless tortures on her. Who was I to deny Tobias the right to avenge the death of his mate? It was just, an act even my mother would likely give leave to.

All this didn't change, however, the two central truths that led to me reaching into my pocket to slide out the tranq dart I had very carefully put there. One, Tobias had been right; the vampires were up to something. Whatever that something was, it spread far beyond Cynthia and Karmarov. Any chance we might have to discover what the tapestry this very loose thread came from looked like might die with Karmarov. And two, if Tobias did succeed in killing the vampire, there was no guarantee that I wouldn't be next.

A streak of red sailed through the lab, pinning Tobias's hindquarter, drawing a yelp from the wolf. His maw rose, dropping Karmarov's arm, an appendage that now was a shredded, mangled collection of rent flesh and purple sinew, looked down his back, and then to me. With the gun still held out in front of me, there was no denying from where the shot had come. I saw confusion fill his eyes, betrayal. The emotions evident in his character hit me in the stomach as good as a fist. Leaving the vampire behind, the wolf rounded, a fearsom growl in my direction as he pulled limbs refusing to comply beneath him.

Karmarov stumbled to his feet, trying to push the torn bits of his arms still attached to the bone into some sort of submission. "Quick, Geri, leave! I'll take care of this."

Take care of this. Those four words confirmed in no uncertain terms that this project, whatever it was, didn't begin and end with this lab. Someone was going to hold Karmarov accountable. Someone was going to want to know what happened.

"What will you tell them about Cynthia?"

He pointed to Kara's body. "The prisoner was able to escape when her moon madness finally set in, and overpowered Cynthia."

I looked to the pile of fur and paws, the slow rise and fall of Tobias's chest. "And him?"

Prof. Karmarov shook his head. "I don't know. They knew we were trying to capture the mate who had followed Cynthia from England when she brought over Kara. I can just say that we were unsuccessful in apprehending him. It doesn't really matter, does it? I saw it in his eyes when he had me pinned. He's on the edge of losing his humanity. Come sunrise, he'll stay trapped in his wolf form. Sooner or later, one of your kind will come for him. If there is a god and mercy still in this world, it will be sooner."

"So what, we just let him go, more animal than man, in a city full of people? You don't know wolves like I do, professor. His instinct will drive him to seek out a remote place. Between here and where that ends up being, however, will be thousands of people. Anyone he perceives to be the slightest threat, he'll kill."

The professor squared his jaw. "The only other alternative is that either you or I kill him first. There's no need for you to have more blood on your hands. I'll do it."

Desperation made my actions bold and movements swift. "Don't!" I bellowed, surprising myself as much as Karmarov with my strength as I jerked him back. "There's another solution."

"I don't encourage keeping a lupified werewolf in the dungeon."

"Not that either. There's a chance that I can still save him from going permanently moon mad. Professor, you saved my life tonight. I still don't understand why. If I leave for twenty minutes, can I trust that no harm will come to this werewolf?"

"Why, what are you going to do with him?"

I shook my head. "I'm still not sure if I can trust you. But if I come back and Tobias is unharmed, then I know I can start trying."

The vampire's eyebrow arched. "And what if you come back to find him dead?"

"Then it will be no worse fate for him."

Karmarov's cold corpse fingers sent a chill through me when they landed on my shoulder, squeezing gently. "I will do him no harm. You have my word. Now go, do whatever you need to do. As for Kara, I will put her in the morgue below. If you're able to save her mate, he can bury her properly when he's ready."

"Thank you, Professor."

"It's the least I can do, Miss Kline."

Amy glared at me, totally unimpressed by my sudden presence.

"So you finally stopped smooching up Jess long enough to come home and change your clothes, huh?"

"What?"

My blonde roommate stretched across the kitchen counter, taking her phone out of her purse. After a few flicks of her screen, she read aloud, "'Amy – OMG, finally happened with Jess. I'll be staying at his place for a while. Text me if you need anything. P.S. He was really, really good.'"

A wave of disgust filled me, and I slammed the door.

Amy's spine straightened. "So I take it that it didn't end well."

"I didn't sleep with Jess," I declared as I peeled off my shirt and headed for my closet. "He stole my phone."

And knocked me out. And took me prisoner on behalf of his vampire master.

"We broke up." It was as close to the truth as I was willing to take her.

Amy's voice was lined with suspicion. "So, then, where have you been for the last three days?"

What was I going to say? It wasn't like I could tell her the truth. With Cynthia dead, I didn't think that Amy would be in any immediate danger. Sure, Karmarov might still turn out to be playing me, but even if that was true, that meant that, for the moment, he wasn't about to strike out against my roommate and risk losing my trust. If Tobias was still alive when I got back to the lab, then I had zero doubt Amy would be safe while I was gone.

It felt like a layer of my skin came off with my bra. God, I wish I had time for a shower. Amy didn't bat an eyelash at seeing me half-naked. She'd learned very early on that I didn't consider nudity that big of a deal.

"I was with, um…"

Suddenly, her face exploded into a grin. "Oh, my god. You were with him, weren't you? The guy from the alley?"

Sure, why not. "Yup, you caught me."

"So you did lose your v-card?"

I slithered into a white t-shirt and some cargo pants. "I still don't know why that concerns you so much, but no."

Braiding my hair, I managed to dive into the bathroom and out of her sight long enough to weave my grandmother's silver blade into a newly tied braid.

"Then, what were you doing for the last three days with him?"

"Comforting him. His wife died."

"His wife? Whoa, you mean he's married?"

"Not anymore." I grabbed a rucksack out of my closet. The weapons within clanked and pinged as metal and wire jingled. "Amy, I'm going to be gone a few days. If anyone comes here looking for me, just say I'm away at a concert or something, okay? The last few days were really stressful. I need to go offline and relax."

"You sure nothing's wrong, Geri? You're acting really strange."

"I'm sure. Once I get where I'm going, I'll see if I can cancel out my old phone and get a new number. Once I do, I'll let you know what it is."

When the doors opened into the lab, a tightness that I'd refused to acknowledge melted. Tobias's wolf, sitting in the middle of the floor, breathed easy. If not for the destruction still evident around him, no one would be the wiser than anything was out of place.

Well, other than a werewolf sleeping in the middle of a science lab.

Karmarov's eyes found me across the room. He sat on the floor, back to the wall, with his legs out in front of him. His black hair with gray outbursts remained disheveled, and a certain weariness in his eyes made me wonder how much the events of this evening had taken out of him.

Stepping into the lab, I let the bag at my side fall to the floor. "Jess?"

"I woke him up long enough to place him under my thrall. Towards morning, I'll have him move out to one of the benches in the college courtyard and change his memories. He'll think he went to a frat party and drank too much. The last few months, just mundane memories of scanning slides. The fact that they were samples of slayers would be an inconvenient truth for him to recall."

I swallowed. "And what will he remember about me?"

Karmarov's eyes narrowed. "It wasn't entirely fake, you know. Yes, he may have been acting on Cynthia's orders to cozy up to you, but the man I saw with you isn't too different from the man he'd actually be without her control. In fact, I could make him believe he's in love with you. You'd practically have yourself a devoted slave."

A bittersweet sting hit the back of my throat. Would the fact that Jess's feelings were nothing more than subterfuge change the feelings I had grown to have for him? After all I had been through the last few days, wouldn't it be worth it to have Karmarov do the very thing he offered to do, just so I could have the satisfaction of engineering a very embarrassing, public break-up?

But when I looked to Tobias and remembered what he'd gone through to try and save his mate, I knew my answer. I wouldn't make a mockery of real love that way.

"It's better that he forgets everything about me. I've betrayed my family secrets too much as it is." I turned to Tobias. "Can you help? I pulled my truck up to the receiving dock downstairs. I don't think I'm strong enough to carry him all on my own."

A smile bloomed on Karmarov's face. "Of course." Without the slightest bit of struggle, the vampire stood, crossed to the slumbering werewolf, and scooped him up. "If I can ask, Miss Kline, if your plan fails, will you kill him yourself?"

I shook my head. "I'm not allowed to kill a wolf without the leave of the matron in whose region it is. Plus, I don't think I'm capable. I'm still a nascent."

"No, Miss Kline. You are so much more than that. More than you understand. Perhaps, more than I understand."

As the elevator doors closed us in, my voice became so much smaller than my confidence. "When I come back to Chicago in a few days, will you tell me what you mean by that?"

"No, all I have are theories, and misinforming you could have tragic consequences. But I promise you, if the evidence ever makes itself clear, I will not hesitate."

TWENTY-NINE

Night, black and beautiful and a salve to my nerves, enveloped us all the way along the Lake Michigan coast. I recalled with envy who I'd been when I'd been a southbound traveler along this same route just eight months ago. That Geri bubbled with anticipation, fizzed with pride at having finally escaped her destiny and her calling. The person I was now bore the shame of that nearsighted optimism. I kept thinking back to the confusion evident on Tobias's face, confusion that reflected my own at the inability to sense the presence of his mate. Had I listened to my mother and taken my rites, would my abilities have been heightened so much that I might have picked up on the fact Kara was imprisoned a few floors below Karmarov's lab? Brünhild had been right about my ability to lure wolves – at least, given how it now seemed clear that I had done just that with Tobias, drawing him to the very heart of the Browning building when Kara and I needed him most, what could I have done with the full scope of my abilities unleashed?

Otherwise deserted roads were dotted at intervals with truckers and the occasional minivan. Outside of Gaylord, I stopped to gas up. After grabbing an anemic-looking ham sandwich from the cooler, I pulled off into the shadows of the parking lot. In the bed of my truck, covered by a tarp, Tobias looked more like a bear I'd bagged and loaded up instead of the massive red wolf he was. Karmarov said the tranq should keep him down the entire trip, but he didn't know werewolves like I did. Open brown eyes met mine. If he could do more than eye me, he made no attempt. Not that I expected it. The body may have survived, but Tobias's soul was DOA. He'd probably hate me for what I was about to attempt, but I couldn't not try. I pulled the syringe from the glove compartment and gave Tobias just enough of a dose for him to sleep off the last few hours.

Not too much. When we got where we were going, I'd need him awake.

But more than that, I'd need to hope that Cody's father would hear me out.

Once we passed the forty-fifth parallel, speed limits became mere suggestions. The blue glow of the clock dash affirmed what I could already feel instinctively; we were running out of time. Inside, I could feel the pull of the moon towards the horizon, despite the fact that a frigid mist and clouded sky greeted us as we crossed Big Mac and touched down in the Upper Peninsula. By the time the highway devolved from the eight-lane monster at the bridge, to the two-lane country road dotted at intervals with potholes and roadkill, I had officially entered panic mode. What was I going to do if I didn't make it? What would I do with a moon mad, permanently lupified werewolf once we got to Paradise?

I didn't have to wonder. The moment my mother found out that Tobias was on her turf – and she would find out – he was a dead wolf walking.

A faint glow of pink already tickled the horizon when I pulled into the Paradise Pack commune, and with it, another realization. Holy shit, what was I doing going into pack territory on a full moon? Just because an alpha maintained the ability to shift back to his human form during a night such as this didn't change the fact that the other wolves couldn't. A nascent hood wandering into a pack of inebriated animals? Stupid. Doing that while dragging a strange wolf into very claimed and established territory? Potentially suicidal.

But as I slammed the car door, leaving the headlights on to provide illumination to the landscape before me, I could hear a few dozen wolves just beyond the forest's edge, gathered close to see what idiot had come into their territory on a full moon. It didn't take long for the first of them to emerge from the forest. No doubt they had heard a car approach, but whether or not they recognized it as mine, I couldn't say. Once, my rust-kissed truck had been a common sight in this area. I stopped by on my way home from work three or four times a week. The Paradise Pack had every right to hate me; I was the daughter of the hood matron who controlled their region with fire and ice. But to them, I'd always just been little Geri Kline, Cody's girlfriend.

A grey-and-black-pelted wolf with deep black eyes made no sound as he trotted toward me. About ten feet away, he stopped, cocked his head, and let out one gentle yip.

"Rick!" I dropped to my knees, forgetting all trepidation. Any tension I still felt eased when the pack's beta nestled up to me and placed his maw on my shoulder, the werewolf-to-human version of a hug. I pulled back and held his head in my hands. "Rick, where's Mr. Ryland? I need to talk to him. Like, man-to-man talk, and it can't wait for sunrise."

Rick turned his head to the edge of the forest, where the silhouette of another pack member shifted from animal to human. At first, the muscular frame and youthful features threw me for a loop. Werewolves did tend to age well, but Cody's dad was in his mid-sixties. Even for a supernatural creature, the alpha's appearance challenged my memory. As the figure stepped into the direct beams of my truck's headlights, however, the understanding of who stood before me sent me scuttling back.

"Cody?"

I had often pictured what it would be like to see my ex-boyfriend again after the way things had ended between us, with him telling me he wanted me to be happy, and me knowing that, having lost him to a she-wolf with whom he'd been his father to bond, I probably never would be. In those visions, I'd never pictured myself shrinking back, scared of his hostility, of his anger. The Cody who fixed me in his acidic glare now didn't want happiness for me; he wanted me dead.

As though picking up on the vibe flowing between us, Rick rounded on all fours, a droning, warning growl rumbling in his chest. At least I still had the beta's affections, even if my ex apparently wanted to kill me.

A scowling Cody turned to his uncle. "I'm not going to hurt her, Rick! Back yourself down."

I did a double take as I watched the beta whimper, his ears falling back over his head. Suddenly, the truth of why Cody was able to shift back to his human form became painfully clear.

"Your dad?"

His brow flinched. "Ask your mother."

"I try to avoid her at all costs." I didn't know what I expected by admitting it. Would he think I was disavowing my family, my clan, my kind? How would that change the way Cody saw me? Did it matter? "I'm so sorry, Cody. I didn't know."

"Yeah, well when you left, you made sure to do it completely, didn't you?"

Such disdain, such bitterness.

"What do you want, Geri?" he asked, getting to the point. "And why do you have an unconscious wolf in the bed of your truck?"

Right, stay focused. Given how much contained anger rolled off of Cody, taking my chances he wouldn't order me chased off the land or even worse, hunted down, might be stupid. I rounded to the back of the truck and untied the ropes holding down the tarp.

"This is Tobias Somfield. He's a lone wolf, turned away from his pack in northern England. His mate was kidnapped three months ago. He's been in Chicago since then, looking for her."

"Three months?" Cody asked, his muscles uncoiling themselves as his arms fell to the side. "Is he…"

"He was showing signs of lunacity before the moon pushed him into his wolf last night," I confirmed. "I came here because you're his last hope. If he's still without a pack when the sun rises, he's likely trapped forever, and we both know what that means."

Cody turned to the lightening sky. "But that's just minutes away."

"Which doesn't give you long to make this decision," I said, pulling off the tarp. "If you don't accept him, and given that I've brought him into my mother's territory, it's likely she'll order his execution as soon as she discovers he's here. I want you to know, however, that I will assume full blame. If she orders his death, I will give it to him mercifully."

The Paradise Pack alpha took turns examining the wolf in question, and me for signs of insanity. "You said he came looking for his mate. Did he find her?"

I nodded. "Yes. Unfortunately, it was too late. She died last night."

I could fill out the details later.

Behind us, Rick leapt lithely into the bed of my truck and nosed Tobias. A moment later, the wolf bared his teeth, huffing. Though I was adept at reading the general context of wolf communication, I couldn't grasp a word-to-word conversation the way a real pack member could. Whatever Rick said to Cody, the latter's temper flared again.

"Why does he smell like vampires?"

No. I was absolutely not going to open up that conversation when Tobias literally had minutes between him and lunacity. "Accept him in this pack, and I'll tell you everything. Cody, the sun's going to rise any minute. Whatever your feelings for me, whatever my mother has done to you, you know me. Last night, Tobias lost the single most important person in the world to him. I know what that feels like. Please, don't make him lose whatever humanity he can hope to have after enduring that too."

My words hit him between the eyebrows. Cody's forehead wrinkled. He wasn't to blame for what had happened between us, just as I wasn't to blame for what did. Still, some small sliver of guilt must have remained. I only prayed now it was a big enough piece to wedge its way into his sense of compassion.

"Fine," he huffed after a few moments. "But you know how this works. I can't just decide he's mine and that's that. He has to accept me. He has to acknowledge me as his alpha, and given that he's passed out—"

I dashed to the glove compartment before Cody could even get through the rest of the sentence. The second shot that Karmarov had provided me lay within, a drug he promised me I should administer only if I wanted Tobias "to go from unconscious to ready to run a marathon in ten seconds flat." He also advised me that I should probably stand clear of the werewolf the second the drug was administered, for my own safety. As I plunged the needle into Tobias's shoulder, however, ten seconds became two.

The English wolf leapt to all fours without time for me to even jump down, throwing me from the back of the truck. Rick took guard over me as Tobias, confused and lackadaisical, fixed me in his sight, his maw wet with saliva, his hackles raised.

I couldn't comprehend the eruption of fur before me. In the time it took me to blink twice, Cody had shifted back to his wolf, throwing the red wolf off balance, knocking him to the ground. Fear and fangs vied for power, but Tobias was no match for the alpha. They'd barely begun when Tobias yelped, letting himself be pinned to the ground just as the first rays of dawn cut through the unfurling canopy of spring above.

I gasped when rough hands and strong arms surrounded me, caging me from behind. My nerves frayed, my patience shot, my instincts cried out to fight. But when the familiar scent reached me, and I understood who held me from behind, all vigor evaporated.

Rick Ryland's voice was a calming salve. "I hope this isn't too awkward, given that I'm naked and everything, but damn it, kid, I was worried about you."

I couldn't help but let out a small laugh. "I'm trying to ignore that fact."

Seeing wolves naked was one thing. Feeling one brush up against me from behind, even if he was practically like family, was a whole different basket of fish.

Rick backed away, tapping me on the shoulders. "Come on, then. Cody's going to need a little time with this pup to get him properly obedient."

THIRTY

My soul felt as warm as the cocoa in the mug Rick gave me as I sat at his kitchen table. "So Tobias accepted Cody as his alpha?"

"After a few four-lettered words, yes." He took a seat across from me, sipping from his own mug of something that smelled suspiciously of whiskey. Since he'd done me the courtesy of putting on some sweatpants and a flannel, I decided not to call him on it. "Colorful language your new wolf has."

"He's not my wolf. He's not my anything."

"And yet, you drove him hundreds of miles in the dead of night to make sure he didn't go moon mad." The beta side-eyed me. "You know most hoods would have just waited for the sunrise then killed him at dawn, don't you? Your mother would be so ashamed if she found out you actually gave a damn about one of us."

"Rick Ryland, you do say the sweetest things."

The door to the garage opened behind me, and I knew who it was just from the look on Rick's face. A beta demurred to no one except his alpha. The way Cody's uncle popped up to his feet and offered his chair like the Queen had just walked in meant it could be no one else. The alpha swiveled the chair, straddling it as he lumbered down. Gone was the anger, filled in around the edges by equal parts resolve and sadness.

"He's taken to the pack," Cody declared. "A few moments more and he would have been gone. I'm still worried. Parts of his humanity may have slipped away, or it could just be that he's in mourning and that's why his mind is so distant. The sadness he feels over losing Kara, it's so palpable, Geri. I don't know if I've done him a favor or not, taking him in."

That Cody knew Kara's name should have surprised me, but it didn't. No doubt Tobias cried it out in his struggles. "You have, Cody, and I can't tell you how much I appreciate it." Without realizing my own actions, I reached across the table. The old familiar thrill ran through me when my hand landed on his, the feeling of possession and pride that I'd reveled in for years when Cody had been mine. Now, however, that feeling carried with it a sense of bitter poison, as though I'd gotten to the front of a long line but only by taking cuts. I pulled back, burying my hands in my lap beneath the table. "I couldn't bring myself to let him go. Not when I knew your dad… you might take him in."

"My dad would have accepted him, too, Geri. He would have done it because you'd be the one to ask him. He loved you. Despite the fact that you're a hood, you were like his own daughter."

A cacophony of unspoken words filled the air between us. The hows, whys, and why nots filled pages of dialogue. Finally, I swallowed hard, and pulled the one written in the boldest font out of the air.

"What happened? Did my mom really do it?"

"Yes! No… I'm not… We're not sure." He ran a hand through his spiky brown hair. "I shouldn't have said that. It's just… Shit, Geri, I'm pissed at you is why. You just upped and left like a fart in the wind. Even if we broke up, you're still my friend. Or at least, I thought we were."

No one had ever labeled Cody as an elegant speaker, but I'd forgotten how he could cut right to the chase in a blink. Probably helped make him a good alpha, frankly.

"I'm sorry, but in my defense, the last time I saw you it was the morning after you mated Lisa, which was also the morning after you asked me to marry you, so…"

"Did you think I was lying when I told you that you were still my best friend?" The pain in his heart became water in his eyes. "You know I had no control over the decision to mate with Lisa. And then when my dad died… You loved my dad almost like you really were his daughter. I expected more of you."

Unanswered phone calls from my father weighed heavy on my mind. Papi had never been a fan of texting, and my voice mail had long ago filled up with his attempts to talk me into returning home.

"I didn't know. If I had… But that's no excuse, Cody. You're right. I should have at least talked to Rick, or even my cousin Markus. I'm sorry. I'm so incredibly sorry, and soon I want to take the proper time to sing his song at the moon."

The corner of Cody's mouth quirked when I'd offered to perform a werewolf mourning rite. "You're not a wolf, Geri."

I kicked him under the table, reviving a tiny bit of our old camaraderie. "Hey, aren't you the one who said I was like his daughter? I might not hit all the right notes. Hell, I might even accidentally yelp some four-lettered words in Lupinese, but I'll remember him in the way he would have wanted. Now—" I leaned forward, folding my hands and placing them on the table. "My mom. Do you really think she might have had something to do with what happened?"

"Your mom keeps such a tight leash on everything, it's hard to imagine something happening that Brünhild Kline doesn't know about. Dad disappeared right before Easter. Your mom said as long as he wasn't posing a danger to himself or others, it wasn't any of her concern. That was six weeks ago. Three weeks ago we… We know when an alpha or our mates die, Geri. I can't explain it, it's instinct somehow. We knew he was gone, and I took his place as alpha."

"I should have been here." I already loathed the fact that Kara's blood was on my hands. Now did I have to accept Mr. Ryland's too?

"What would you have been able to do?" Cody asked. "I can't even say something went wrong. Maybe he had a heart attack out in the woods somewhere. Maybe he got caught by a poacher. Maybe he went out fishing alone on Superior and got caught in a storm."

"And maybe what happened to him is the same thing that happened to Tobias's mate," I interjected.

That stopped Cody dead. "So what happened? He won't talk about it. Can't blame him. It's still too fresh."

"Some vamps are running genetic experiments. I don't know exactly why, but they're altering wolf DNA."

"Vamps?" Cody leaned back in his seat, crossing his meaty arms over his chest. "Not good. But we haven't picked up on any scent around here that would suggest vampires have been traipsing about the woods."

A long screech and the knock of wood on wood drew both our attentions. I looked over Cody's shoulder to see Tobias, looking the most ragged I had ever seen him, come through the door. He wiped a dirty hand over an oily face and stopped short when he saw Cody at the table.

"Alpha," he said, growing smaller where he stood. "Apologies, I was looking for the hood. Beta told me she was in here."

My ex-boyfriend stood, vacating the chair and motioning for the newest member of his pack to take a seat. "I don't know how things operated in your old pack, Tobias, but in this one, we're family. You call me Cody, and my uncle's name is Rick. You go around giving him a superiority complex, I'm worried you'll have to settle up with Aunt Kathy."

Tobias became the very model of obeisance, a coat that, as the beta of his old pack, I was sure he didn't feel fit him. "Yes, Alpha. I mean… Cody." His eyes flashed to me, then back to the floor. "Can I speak with the hood?"

Cody looked to me for acknowledgment, asking my permission with his eyes. I gave him a silent nod.

"Her name is Geri. And while she's a hood, and not pack…" Warmth filled his expression, pouring out of him and into me. "…she's as close as you can get. Don't go giving her any titles, either. She's already carrying around one that bogs her down enough as it is. Geri—" Cody leaned over, putting a hand on my shoulder. "—I'm going to be right outside the door listening. You feel in any danger at any point, you just say our old catch phrase, okay?"

Tobias eased once Cody left the room, but the old determination that had once made every movement of his bold and purposeful had left him. His body surrendered to the seat, dropping like a bag of flour. He steepled his hands and leaned into a prayer pose. I gave him room, both physically and emotionally, sitting back in my chair and waiting for him to talk first.

Finally, it came out. "Why didn't you just kill me?"

I labored to keep my tone even. "Because that's not who I am."

"That's exactly who you are. You're a hood. Hell, if you'd let me make it to sunrise, I couldn't have even held it against you. I was on the edge, I felt it. But you've pulled me back to live like this." His hands reached out in either direction, motioning broadly to the modest kitchen with mustard yellow counters and pea green synthetic floors. "In a foreign land, with a pack I don't know, without the mate whom I love. You don't know what it feels like, Kline, to lose the one whose life gave yours purpose."

Beyond the screen door, Cody half-turned his head, looking over his shoulder.

"I know a little bit about how that feels." I swallowed down my memories. "Listen, Tobias, I can't pretend to understand fully what you've gone through, but if nothing else comes out of it, know this: you were right. There is a group of vampires, and they are up to something. What it is exactly, I don't know yet. But with your help, I'd like to find out."

"My help?" The bitterness in his voice poisoned the sarcastic laugh he let out. "Why should I help, when I repeatedly came to you, only to be turned away? I saved your life twice, and the most I got from you in return was 'sorry, I know I'm technically a hood, but I don't actually want to be a hood, so you're on your own.'"

His sharp words hit their mark, making my insides squirm as my sense of righteousness attempted to claw its way out of a slew of guilt. "You're right. I have no right to ask for your help, and even less to expect it. But in that case, let me help you, Tobias. Kara was murdered. Let me help you avenge her."

"I don't believe in all that life-for-a-life bollocks."

"No, then what about two lives?" When he just stared blankly at me, I grew a pair of my own bollocks and told him the truth. "When I was in the dungeon of Browning Hall, Cynthia showed me the body of another wolf. She said it was the alpha of a pack from England. That, combined with the fact that you're his spitting image, would suggest to me she's the one who killed your brother."

His face cycled through a slew of emotions: surprise, frustration, confusion, anger, and then confusion again.

"But Cynthia is already dead. You killed her, I remember that. Other than Karmarov, there is no one else to hold accountable for what happened to my brother and Kara."

"I think Karmarov is on our side," I said. "He saved my life. He could have killed you easy, and he didn't. And while I'm not exactly forgetting that he helped throw both your mate and me in a dungeon, we need his help. There's something bigger going on here. Something that goes beyond my college campus and a few vampires in Chicago. What we need to do is find out who they are and exactly what they're up to. And then, once we know that, we can hold every one of them to the fire. Until we do that, every wolf is a possible target for their experimentation."

"You're talking like a hood. Like a real hood, one who actually wants to protect us rather than kill us. I thought you had no interest in your birthright?"

"I don't. But I got blood on my hands now. Kara's blood. If I had listened to you, I might have been able to save her. If I don't listen to the voice in my head telling me now that this is nowhere near over, who knows how many more will die? But I'm still a nascent. I don't have the strength or the skills to go this alone. I need your help."

Tobias leaned back in his chair, contemplation in his gaze. "I'd need permission of my alpha."

"Done!" Cody shouted out from outside with such ferocity, we both flinched.

Tobias lowered his voice. Why, I'm sure he couldn't say. He'd have to know that Cody would still be able to hear us. "He accepted me in his pack, but I have to wonder why. He seems eager to get rid of me."

"It has nothing to do with you," Cody said, forgoing all illusions of privacy and coming back in through the screen door. "Until Geri takes her rites, she hasn't a chance against a wolf that really wants to do her harm. I doubt she'd do much better against a vamp. Once upon a time, before hoods and slayers, there was just us and them. We were the vamps' balance. Maybe it's time we try that out again."

An invisible ball of awkwardness bounced on the table between us. Lucky for me, Tobias wasn't about to correct his new alpha in front of company, and I wasn't about to give the FYI to my ex-boyfriend that validated his – well, alpha male attitude.

"I swear to you, Cody, I will protect her with my life." Then, under his breath, he added, "Again."

Cody let the jibe go and turned to me. "Geri, once he gets rested up, he's all yours. But he's been through a lot and he's in mourning. He needs a little time. Can you wait to go back?"

I shook my head. "I'm still worried for my roommate. She's a Huey, but this whole mess first started when a vamp tried to pick her up in a bar. It could have been coincidence, but I'm not sure. I need to make sure she's okay. Plus, I have final exams in a few weeks, and I haven't studied at all yet."

"Still bound and determined to do the college thing, then." The alpha grinned. "Good. If you just upped and gave up because you had lone wolves and vampires after you, you just wouldn't be my Geri."

I bit my tongue, reminding him that, as a wolf mated to another wolf, I wasn't his anything anymore.

"You can't go back alone, though. Take Kimmy."

My eyes went wide. "WHAT?"

This time, it was the alpha who flinched. "Come on, Kim's great. She's been wanting to get away for a while. If you think your roommate wouldn't care if you had a houseguest, that is."

"But she's so…" Loud. Awkward. Rambunctious. Muscular. Cody's cousin on his mother's side remained the only girl in the history of our high school football team to get the MVP trophy. "Kim."

Cody considered that a moment before making a counteroffer. "If you prefer, I can send Lisa. But I warn you, you're not exactly her favorite person."

"No, Kim will be fine." Much better than your mate. "I'm sure Amy won't mind a bit. And if I tell her that Kim and I are dating, she might even insist she move in."

About Kendrai Meeks

Kendrai Meeks was deported from the American Midwest after graduating college, and held against her will since in California. She *really* hates sarcasm. She first published in 2011, and has since put out books in romance and science fiction. In 2017, she decided to return to her first love, urban fantasy. She has also been a featured speaker on a number of conference and industry panels on topics ranging from Fanfiction, to Audiobooks, to Serialized Fiction. She is a world music devotee and loves to travel (just hates to fly – a conflict, for certain). She enjoys twisting the extant into the exceptional, often basing her work on historical themes or legendary folk tales and mythology.

Acknowledgments

The best part of this new adventure has been the friends I have made in the process. I want to especially give thanks to Laura and Dan Martone, N.E. Montgomery, Tom Hansen, Freddie Kim, Audrey Sharpe, Adam Myhr, R.R. Roberts, J.S. Morin, Marcelle Liemant, Matt R., and my other fellow Journeymen.

Thanks for the guidance from Jamie Davis, Amy Teegan, and Christine Niles. A second round of applause for Amy for kicking ass as part of my editing team, and to Colleen Vanderlinden for rounding out that team.

A HUUUUGGGGEEEE thanks to Tammi. I mean, like huge. A big, freaking mountain of hugeness on which little thank-you unicorns hop and sing and procreate to breed even more adorbs little thank-you offspring, thus adding to the circle of huge.

Many thanks to those in my non-writing life whose support make my writing life possible: Ann Grimes, Andrea Kuduk, Denise Murphy, and Maneesh Agrawala.

And a special thank you to Elizabeth Hunter, Scott Hoffman, and Mandy Murat. These people are the reason that in my darkest days, I can eventually find the light.

THE RED CHRONICLES - BOOK TWO: RELINQUISHED

No, it can't be. Not now!

The feeling I got when an unknown wolf approached me was like the one you got as a rollercoaster ticked and clicked its way up the first big hill. A wolf I did know, however? It was the ride down, the pulse-spiking, wind-whipping rush of adrenaline that prompted your fight or flight instincts.

I'd just gone down Space Mountain, a plunge in my gut so rapid and pulverizing it could only be one particular wolf who stood on the other side of my door.

"Huff, puff, Geri."

My backpack thudded to the floor. The last time I saw Tobias had been when I'd left him behind with the pack in Paradise, just a few days after I'd barely gotten him there in time to save his life. An echo of the guilt I felt then formed in my gut, like a mother leaving her disabled child in the care of a nurse. I knew it was the right place for him, but I still felt the burden of his care. In the intervening time, the worst of his pain had ebbed, but even now, standing before him, his conflicted feelings mixed with my own. Part of him wanted to cry at the sight of me; I was the only one beside Igor who had been present when his mate died. We would forever be bound by that tragedy. Yet, reality didn't bow to grief. I was still a hood; he was still a wolf. Our instincts drove us to hate each other.

I didn't want to hate Tobias, but I couldn't be seen as weak and sympathetic either. For a hood to appear weak to a wolf was to open herself to danger. She lived thereafter at his leisure.

Tobias's face crumpled when I threw open the door, seething. "It wasn't an order, you know."

I cocked my head to the side. "What are you talking about?"

"The huffing and the puffing," he answered.

I took a moment to draw back my rage at his sudden appearance. How dare he just show up out of nowhere, when he had no right to be so soon a widower and away from the comfort and support of his pack. How dare he bring this baggage back to my door so soon.

"Why in the hell are you here?"

He pushed past me, and for once in my life, I wished the rule about not being able to enter a home without an invitation applied to werewolves instead of vampires.

"Well, right this second, I'm here because I have to piss. Where's your loo?"

My hand lashed out, indicating the door. Without so much as a thank you or a word of explanation, Tobias dove for the "loo," closed the door, and proceeded to moan as he relieved himself.

"Did Cody send you?" I yelled through the wooden slab covered in layers and layers of paint.

"God, this feels so good. I drove here straight from Paradise, didn't stop." With another grunt, the grotesque virtuoso urination stopped, the toiled flushed, and the faucet came on. "By the way, whose idea was it to name that bloody little puissant tourist trap Paradise? I'm thinking it was the same dullards who came up with Greenland. The waterfalls are nice, though."

"I repeat, why are you here?"

The door opened to reveal the werewolf using Amy's frilly pink hand towels to dot the moisture from his hands.

"You're kidding, right?" he asked, a bit of gruff in his timbre. "Remember about a month ago when a certain vampire held you prisoner and killed my mate? And then, how you asked me to help you figure out what was going on, so it doesn't happen to others?"

"Of course, I remember. But you're in mourning. I can feel the sadness on you. It's … sticky, heavy. Vampires are immortal, they're not going anywhere. The problem will still be there once you've taken the proper time to…"

"To what? Get over Kara?" he demanded. "That's never going to happen. I might as well be here, trying to keep it from happening to others."

All at once, every muscle in my body went tense. "Has it happened to anyone else?"

"Not in Paradise," Tobias said. "Once Cody relayed what had happened to me and you down here, your mum suddenly snapped to attention. She's been running perimeter checks around the packlands twenty-four, seven. And speaking of your mum…"

I'd never stopped to think about it, but as soon as Brünhild Kline was aware a foreign wolf had suddenly joined the pack, she'd probably dragged him in for questioning. "Did she hurt you?"

"No, but I had to bite my own paw to keep from hurting her. I've never heard a mother talk about her own daughter the way she talks about you. What exactly did you do to piss her off so much?"

"It seems to have started with my birth, and went downhill from there," I answered. "Don't forget, she named me after the most heinous traitor in our bloodline, in any bloodline. Just in case you were wondering if Gerwalta is a common name among hoods… it isn't."